Late August, 2(

Ch

The sun was shining as the train zipped past green fields and olive groves, playing a soft percussive melody; a chook-a-chook of promise and opportunity...

'Are you pregnant?'

'What?'

'Bambino!'

I was suddenly jolted out of my peaceful reverie and turned from the window to see a typically Italian *Mamma* gesturing to my stomach and smiling warmly so the creases in her face scrunched together like brown paper.

'No, I just like pizza' I replied chirpily, a gormless grin on my face.

She laughed and pointed to her own stomach (which was three times the size of mine I must add) as she wistfully breathed *'ahh, Si, Signorina*. Me too. Twins for me.'

I laughed awkwardly and nodded before continuing to gaze at the moving landscape.

Of course, I was absolutely mortified. *Did I really look pregnant?* I knew I had little bit of a pudgy middle but surely I didn't look pregnant. *Did I?*

Being mistaken for an expectant mother was an even harder blow to take considering I'd spent most of the summer running up hills and drinking protein shakes in a last-ditch attempt to achieve the no-airbrushing-needed 'bikini body' which every women's mag raved about. Clearly, I was still a long way off.

On this day however, nothing could get me down. I may have been fat, I may have felt unprepared, but this day marked the beginning of what I would later say was the most influential year of my life. I could sense that even then.

After catching a flight from Dublin, I'd boarded the train at Verona and was on my way to Bologna where I'd be attending the university for a year as part of a foreign study exchange program called 'Erasmus.' I was nauseous with excitement. I'd only studied Italian for two years but I was already in love. Every word was a soft note to my ear and sentences arranged themselves like sweet romantic melodies. Even the most mundane conversation could seem like a sonata in Italian. *'Che bella'* I whispered as we passed hills draped in fig trees set against a pale crimson sky.

It was only just getting dark as the train pulled into Bologna so I could still admire the burnished red and half crumbling buildings, the quaint alleyways, the endless arcades. At first sight it seemed like an ancient civilisation which had lain untouched for centuries, perfectly preserved in a spellbound slumber yet still pulsing with vitality.

I dragged my suitcase and other bags across Piazza Maggiore, whilst panting and perspiring profusely, stopping only briefly to admire the impressive yet unfinished marble façade of San Petronio cathedral which stoically watches over the square. I plodded on, heavily laden with books I probably wasn't going to read and my guitar which although not essential, was something I simply couldn't live without.

Eventually I arrived at the end of a particularly narrow street where an open door allowed a pale pool of light to spill onto the cobbles. I took a deep breath, letting my pounding heart slow a little before heaving my luggage across those last two metres and through the doorway.

Here we go – the start of a new adventure

'Ciao, Buona Sera.'

A tanned young man with impressive biceps greeted me, smiling and leaning nonchalantly over a mahogany counter. As I slid my passport across the desk, our hands briefly brushed against each other. I quickly snatched mine back, balling it into a nervous fist.

'I'm Roberto' he said, giving me a sly wink. I blushed and promptly looked down at my feet, averting my gaze from his deep chestnut eyes. My mouth twitched with glee.

I may look pregnant, but I've still got it.

As Roberto showed me to my room, he insisted on helping with my suitcase which he was able to easily swing up onto his shoulder as though its only contents were candy floss. Ordinarily my pride would have rallied against such a freely given act of kindness; but it had been a long day after all, and I enjoyed the view.

As I followed him up a rickety staircase and down several winding corridors, I noticed some strange pictures on the walls. All around me were examples of psychedelic and absurd artwork, the weirdest being the papier mâché bust of an aboriginal woman with glazed grapes glued on for nipples. This coupled with the black and white floor tiles and garish yellow curtains made me feel as though I'd fallen into a kaleidoscope.

Then someone twisted it. Suddenly my head spun, and I was reminded of my exhaustion following a day of travelling in thirty-degree heat. My stomach lurched and my last thought was *please no* before I vomited in the corridor and all over Roberto's patent leather shoes just as he had turned the key to my room. The colour drained from my face. All I could do was stare blankly at the floor, too horrified to look up.

'*Ahh Signorina*. Don't worry I'll get you some tissues' he said sympathetically but I could tell he was disgusted,

'I'm so sorry' I muttered, eyes fixed firmly on the floor.

Then I jolted, suddenly letting out a piercing shriek.

A large scruffy rat scurried across the floor, through my sick, and continued along the corridor leaving a trail of tiny yellow paw marks.

'*Ah tranquilla signorina.* Why you scream? That's just Giovanni. He's our oldest resident' said Roberto casually. Then he laughed manically for about five minutes before eventually going to get me those tissues.

It took all of my mental willpower not to vomit again, over and over, but somehow, I managed to keep it down. When I finally looked up I noticed a canvas with some words crudely formed out of multi-coloured spaghetti,

'Welcome to Amici Hostel.'

Chapter 2

The next morning I awoke as the sun poured in through jaundiced curtains. I'd barely slept. The bed sheets itched, and I couldn't stop thinking about Giovanni, hoping that he wouldn't scurry back in the night to formally introduce himself. I was in a six bed dorm but the only other person I was sharing with was a Japanese boy who didn't seem to speak English and wore oversized headphones, even when he slept. Some of my initial hope and optimism had certainly drained away. I'd barely been in Italy for twenty-four hours and had already suffered two of the most embarrassing moments of the twenty years I'd lived thus far. *Still, today's a new day - Andiamo.*

In the light of day I could see Amici hostel in all of its glory - all of its filthy glory. The air hung heavy with dust, the walls had dubious stains, and due to weak plumbing, toilet paper wasn't allowed to be flushed so it just gathered in an adjacent bin, piling up in a stagnant heap. I still felt a bit nauseous but decided to venture downstairs for breakfast which was included in the price – a price which I now realised was so cheap for a reason.

Crossing a small courtyard with more surreal artwork (I think I saw a painting of Jesus with bunny ears), I made my way to the kitchen where there was a wicker basket piled high with croissants and a coffee machine on the counter. I hunched down and took a moment to scan the floor for any sign of Giovanni. I couldn't see any droppings but the floor pattern was polka-dot, so it was hard to tell.

'He's more afraid of you ye know'

A distinctive Dublin lilt drifted over my right shoulder.

I spun round to see a short boy with dirty blond hair gathered in a rough top knot, wearing a brightly coloured silk shirt,

'I'm Ronan' he said, extending his hand and grinning mischievously,

'Kerry - nice to meet you.' I replied, gingerly shaking his baby soft hand.

'So, I take it you've met Giovanni too?'

'Aye sure we go down the pub every Friday. He's great craic.'

He glanced down as he swilled his coffee gently in its tiny cup but a smile was creeping up on one side of his mouth.

'What does he drink? A mice-i-to?' I spasmodically blurted out,

Oh God Kerry that one was bad, even for you.

'Ha, no just the odd whisk-er-y or two.'

We both laughed. Ronan's was the kind that rang through a room, cutting the air with its positive energy. I'd never heard a laugh like that before and never have since.

'How long have you been here?' I dared to ask.

My plan had been to stay in a hostel just for a few days till I could find a room to rent but I really couldn't envisage being able to cope with that place for more than a week.

'About a month' he replied casually as he licked a few flecks of pastry off his top lip.

My heart sank. The thought of spending a month there made me want to vomit all over again - everywhere. The croissant I'd picked up suddenly didn't seem so appetising.

'Is it that hard to find accommodation here?' I said, trying to hide the fact that I was on the verge of a panic attack and uselessly fumbling with the coffee machine.

'No, it's just handy and cheap. I work at the Irish bar, The Emerald, round the corner on Via Paradiso most nights and study in the library during the day. It's just a place to sleep like' he said, twitching the corner of his mouth and shrugging his shoulders.

'Ahhhh, fuck' I swore as I pressed a button on the curious contraption which unexpectedly splurted out scalding water.

Wordlessly Ronan took the little metal thingy out of my hands, pressed a button that filled it with ground coffee, pulled down a lever that compressed it before he hitched it up, locked it into place, twisted it like an expert handyman and pressed a button which dispensed an espresso. I felt so inept in the face of such sorcery. Before then coffee for me was just gravelly granules that you poured a kettle over.

'You should probably run that under the cold tap' he added as he handed me my coffee.

I presumed he was referring to my hand but part of me wondered if that could be an extra step in the magic of Italian coffee making.

I gratefully accepted the cup and awkwardly shuffled towards the sink.

'I suppose it's not that bad here.' I said matter of factly, even though I categorically disagreed.

I tried not to think about why the water soothing my hand was a curious shade of brown.

'So, what do you study?' If I'd hazarded a guess I would have said Art. Only a tortured artist would be crazy enough to stay in The Amici out of his own free will.

'Theatre studies, what about you?'

'Italian and French'

'Ah so you're a linguist. Cool' he said, fidgeting a little with the buttons of his shirt.

Ah so you're a method actor, using the Amici hostel as a metaphor for the struggles of a madman in a dystopian plot.

We chatted for a bit more before finishing our croissants and downing our espressos.

Fellow Irish people always seem to meet abroad, it must be kind of magnetism I thought.

As the caffeine zinged my brain to life I pondered on the joys of identifying with a nationality that is simultaneously inescapable and globally adored.

Ronan was from Dublin and I come from a small town on the north coast so to certain people back home I suppose it would seem as though we were poles apart, but to me talking to Ronan was the most natural thing in the world, as though I'd known him my whole life. There was something about him that was calming too, as though just being near him was enough for me to absorb his carefree attitude by osmosis.

'What are ye at this morning?' he asked me expectantly, his eyes sparkling with playfulness.

'I was going to begin my apartment hunt' I replied sullenly. The thought of this grim task filled me with more than a little dread.

'No you're not' He rocked back on his heels slightly and smirked.

'What? Why?' I asked incredulously,

'You're coming up Torre Asinelli with me'

And that was that. About half an hour later I was following Ronan up a narrow stone staircase which seemed to spiral up and up forever, all the way to heaven. In any case, I felt like I was dying. I was panting, red-faced and drenched in sweat. Torre Asinelli is one of two old towers which stand in the centre of Bologna, leaning precariously, collectively known as the 'Due Torri.' The smaller of the two, Torre Garisenda, is too unstable to allow visitors but you can climb to the top of Asinelli for three euros. Yes, I'd paid three euros for this hell!

I hadn't really been able to politely refuse Ronan's 'invitation' though. He'd practically grabbed me by the hand and yanked me out of the hostel. When we'd passed reception Roberto had his feet up on the desk and was slumped back in his chair in deep slumber, a fly poised on the end of his nose. *Maybe he's a mere mortal after all,* I thought, smiling to myself. Then the memory of being sick over him the night before came rushing back. I cringed, half hoping it had all been a bad dream. *I don't think any amount of flirting will make up for that Kerry.* I feared my inner pessimist was right. Of course, Ronan found the story hilarious,

'So, you fancy Rob-dog but you boked all over him. Ha what are ye like!' he said, bounding up the steps two at a time like a Springer Spaniel,

'God...he probably...thinks...I'm...repulsive.'

I could barely form a straight sentence and felt as though all of the air in my lungs was being sucked out by a vacuum. The walls seemed to be closing in on me too. It was all a bit claustrophobic. My panic returned.

'You don't sound great, here have a drink.' Ronan turned to me proffering his water bottle. I greedily took several gulps, instantly feeling better.

'Don't worry we're almost at the top' he said, offering me his hand.

I gladly took it as he helped me climb the last few steps. I imagined I looked like a slightly senile elderly woman who was being taken to bed. *That's a dear Kerry love, up we go.* As we neared the top, the steps appeared increasingly worn and dipped in the middle due to centuries of tread. Then at last we were blinded by the brilliant sunshine and I blinked at a cloudless blue sky. We'd made it.

'Well, what do you think? It was worth it right?'

I had to agree with Ronan. The view was spectacular. Below us an agglomeration of terracotta and burnished red rooftops sprawled out in every direction, pressing into the surrounding hillsides.

I'd read in my guidebook that Bologna was also known as 'La Rossa' – the red one. Now I understood why. It was only from here that I was also able to appreciate how many long, wide streets the city had which seemed to stretch from the centre all the way out to the countryside as though Bologna wasn't a man-made civilisation at all but part of the land itself; a pulsating red fruit.

We asked a loud American tourist to take a picture of us. Ronan swung his arm around me and pulled me closer.

'Say cheese folks' the man boomed.

I smiled as wide as I could, thinking that this would probably be one of the most unattractive photos ever taken of me. My hair was damp and sticking to my face, which by now probably matched the shade of the buildings below. I didn't care though. Not really.

We stared down at the view for a while longer in silence, captivated by the beauty which surrounded us as a welcome breeze brushed past. Ronan had stepped up onto the wall and was leaning precariously over the railing. I half imagined that at any moment he would stretch out his arms, and effortlessly swan dive, taking flight like Peter Pan.

'Did you know that students have a superstition about this tower?' he asked, pulling me out of my reverie,

'No what's that?'

I was intrigued. I'd never really bought into silly things like not walking under ladders, or avoiding cracks on the pavement, but since the age of five I'd always saluted solitary Magpies. My granny once said that they were evil and would curse you if you didn't. My granny was usually right.

'They say that if you come up here before you finish your degree you won't graduate.'

'Now you tell me!' I said in a mock-angry tone.

Part of me was a little worried though. Magpies or not, I wasn't exactly the luckiest person in the world.

'Don't worry, this is my second time up here so I can just take your bad luck and fail twice' said Ronan, smiling that mischievous grin again.

'That would be awfully gallant of you' I said, theatrically flicking my hair and tilting my head to one side.

'Anything for my k-dog' he said jokingly, giving me a brotherly shoulder bump.

But I knew he meant it.

When we'd descended, I remembered that I had to start looking straight away for accommodation. After all, I only had a week before my classes started and I didn't want to have the extra stress of home-hunting then. Ronan sent me in the direction of Piazza Verdi where the walls, bins and lamp posts were all collaged with coloured strips of paper advertising rooms to rent.

I rang a few numbers and made some enquiries in my best Italian but I didn't have much luck. Most of the rooms were already taken or so far out from the centre that they weren't even worth considering. Ideally, I wanted to be as close to the university as possible; for late morning lie-ins, and the bars; for late night stop-outs.

After a while I gave up and just decided to enjoy the gloriously sunny day. I explored a little and wandered through the winding streets, savouring one of those rare moments when one has nowhere particular to be and nothing especially to do. As I walked around the city, passing quaint little book shops and happy couples sharing gelato on terraces, I half felt as though I had just come out of a coma and was experiencing life for the first time. The smell of fresh bread, the sound of an accordion - everything arrested my senses and caught my eye. I was wide awake but I was walking through a dream; a beautiful technicolour dream.

My first two years at university had been more of a nightmare. When I got my A-level results I'd gleefully packed my bags and moved to Manchester, bursting with hope as I began a new chapter. Perhaps I was a little naïve but part of me thought that if I moved away I could leave all my troubles behind on the other side of the Irish Sea. Life doesn't work like that. After a few weeks of my first term I cracked under the pressure.

Trying to fit in, heavy drinking, parties, essays, deadlines – I clung to the stress of it all, letting it bubble under the surface until finally I cracked and found myself in a hospital bed with a searing pain in my throat. People will always tell you that your twenties are the best years of your life but depression isn't ageist. She's a cold mistress who slowly seeps in, wrapping her smoky fingers around your heart at a rate which is barely perceptible until your mind is full of fog and you forget what happiness truly is.

Now the air was clear and the Italian sun beamed down upon me warming every inch of my soul. I stopped for a moment just to breathe, and to look, and to be. On the awning of a little jewellery shop two pigeons were courting; cooing softly, strutting and flapping noisily in that way which pigeons do. I smiled. After spending my fair share of time in darkness it felt good to finally step into the light.

By dusk I found myself back at Piazza Verdi. Ronan said he had a few people he'd like me to meet and Verdi was the nocturnal hang-out to be it seemed.

At night the square took on a whole new life. The place hummed with busy chatter, the clink of bottles and the soft strumming of an out of tune guitar. Groups of young people sat on the ground in large circles whilst Pakistani men ambled back and forth, selling cheap beer,

'*Birra, vuoi birra*?' they chanted. It probably wasn't authentic stuff, but it did the job. A faint smell of weed hung in the air. I followed Ronan as we sat down beside two pale pretty girls and two dark-haired guys in the middle of the square.

'Hi guys, this is K-dog' he announced proudly,

'I'm Kerry' I subtly corrected 'nice to meet you'

I had mixed feelings about my new nickname. On one hand I didn't think it suited me at all and sounded more like the stage name of a second-rate rapper, but then again, I knew that it was meant as a term of endearment; Ronan's own quirky way of saying 'you're stuck with me now.'

'Do you want a beer K-dog?'

One of the boys spoke with a posh London accent and rolled me over a Peroni before I had a chance to reply.

'The name's Bond, Edward Bond, license to flirt' he said, making intense eye contact which unsettled me,

'Aye Teddy boy thinks he's the shit like, but he's not a bad spud' interjected Ronan.

Everyone laughed.

'Ah, um, thanks' I said, 'I'm Kerry - Kerry O'Neil, license to get drunk.'

Everyone laughed again apart from Edward who just smirked and obnoxiously took another swig of his beer. I knew I'd won the battle of wits though and it felt good.

I could have finished that sentence any number of ways really;

License to embarrass herself,

License to be athletically challenged,

License to vomit unexpectedly,

Looking around me though, it would have appeared that I was the only one there who needed official permission to inebriate myself.

'You should come to our flat sometime for a Russian dinner' said one of the girls in a spritely voice. Her name was Anita and the other girl was Tatiana. They both came from the same small town in Russia, Dubrovka, and were there to study Art History for the year. We were all there to study on the Erasmus program actually, apart from Edward who was working full time in a bar and on a post-university gap-year to 'find himself.'

'Yes our Russian dinners are great' added Tatiana, grinning a Cheshire cat smile. She was taller and leaner compared to Anita with long blond hair and a face which glowed with childlike innocence,

'You mean come round for a bottle of vodka'

The other guy who had been silent until then finally spoke.

'The last time I went to one of your Russian 'dinners' I had a three day hangover'

His thick French accent seemed comical and inexplicably out of place. I twisted slightly to the right to face him and was instantly struck by his pale blue eyes which illuminated an otherwise plain face.

'Well, some people just aren't man enough for vodka, stick to your faggot champagne Marc' said Edward scathingly. I drew a sharp breath. The awkward tension was palpable and Anita was now giving him such a death stare that at any second I thought she was going to jump up and punch him square in the jaw. It was the first time I'd seen Ronan look angry too and it really didn't suit him.

'I don't drink champagne' Marc replied flatly. He said nothing more for the rest of the evening.

We sat there drinking beer late into the night. At one point Anita went and bought pizza for everyone. It was crisp, thin and delicious. The air was warm and sweet and I wanted desperately to breath it all in and hold on to everything forever – Anita's pretty smile, Ronan's tuneful laugh, Marc's mysterious sapphire eyes, even Edward's pompous throat clearing.

But it was all just part of another ephemeral memory.

Chapter 3

I spent most of the days which followed persevering in my accommodation search. It wasn't easy to say the least. I went to have a look at a few places but nothing appealed to me. One apartment I viewed had a visible layer of brown scum on the kitchen floor and rotting meat in the fridge which impregnated every room with its stench, attracting flies which buzzed noisily around the net curtains. The landlady looked like an old witch with straggly black hair reaching to her waist and yellowing teeth.

'You want room?' she croaked in the rasping tone of someone who smokes thirty a day.

I politely declined.

Another place I looked at seemed to tick all of the boxes at first. It was close to Piazza Verdi and had a clean and cosy little communal living space complete with a fully equipped rat-free kitchenette. It was a double but I'd shared rooms before at university and didn't mind as long as the other girl respected my privacy and was pleasant enough. When I went in to have a look I saw two beds on either side of a spacious, airy room. On one of them an olive-skinned boy around my age was sprawled out reading a comic book - stark naked. He got up to say hello,

'Hey, my name's Julio' he said, offering his hand for me to shake. I gingerly did so making sure that I kept my eyes on his face and at least an arm's width of distance between our bodies. After a few minutes of stilted small talk with me feigning interest in the posters which covered the walls and Julio seemingly widening his stance as though limbering up to shift into a yoga pose, I eventually made up an excuse to leave, mumbling about some appointment or other. I wasn't a prude but sharing a room with a Mexican nudist was just a step too far.

I spent my evenings mostly at Piazza Verdi with Ronan and co. but sometimes we stayed at the hostel which I discovered actually had quite a nice common room complete with a 1970's style brown sofa and a set top TV with a broken aerial. There was always someone interesting to talk to though and new travellers came and went every day.

One night I got out my guitar and had a jam session with two South Africans who had brought a pair of bongos with them.

'Ag that's a banging instrument' said one guy with scruffy blond hair, freckles and tanned skin,

'Yeah it's lekker, ain't ever seen one like that before' added the other who looked almost identical to the first but was slightly taller and wore a shark-tooth necklace.

They were of course referring to my pride and joy that was my shiny lilac guitar. It came everywhere with me, always at the ready for a quick sing along or spontaneous song writing sesh. Back in Manchester I occasionally played in local bars, the fear vibrating in my fingers but not showing in my voice. It was all worth it for the after-buzz.

'Alright Kerry let's get this jol started' enthused South African number one.

I looked around. There were a few other people in the room including a Swedish couple silently playing cards at a table in the corner and a wild-eyed black man with dreadlocks who was staring at us expectantly. I suddenly felt a little nervous as I often did in front of intimate audiences but nevertheless I cleared my throat and began to sing the first song which came into my head,

'In the jungle, the mighty jungle the lion sleeps tonight...' I started out softly but gradually gained confidence and momentum. Then the South African boys joined in, adding harmonies as one of them slapped the bongos and the other clicked his fingers. By the time we got to the 'a wim-a-ways' the whole room was joining in including an old woman with hairs on her chin who whistled cheerfully and Ronan who was rhythmically tapping the table with a spoon.

Roberto walked into the room half way through and starting filming us. He later uploaded the video to the Amici hostel website to serve as a sort of advert to lure in potential guests. *God help those poor unsuspecting souls.*

I couldn't deny though that the Amici had a sort of ramshackle charm about it and I grew accustomed to its ways in the same way you can get used to an inconspicuous hole in the crotch of your jeans or a crack on your phone screen.

One night when we came back late from Piazza Verdi Ronan said he had something to show me in the kitchen.

'You have to be fast though' he said intently.

I wondered what on earth he was on about. Then he showed me that if you quickly opened the door to the kitchen and almost simultaneously flicked the light switch it was possible to catch a glimpse of a few cockroaches before they scuttled away beneath the cupboards.

'Speedy wee skitters aren't they?'

I nodded slowly in agreement. If I hadn't been tipsy and slightly high from a joint we'd shared about half an hour before I probably would have been repulsed.

Instead, I just gazed at Ronan, wide-eyed and woozy as though he had just opened my eyes to the most magical secret in the world.

I hadn't seen Giovanni again since our first fated meeting the night I arrived. That is until I woke up early to take a shower one morning. There was only one bathroom and the queue could get quite long so I had decided to get up at six am to beat everyone to it.

Shuffling in with my feet bound in plastic bags (a precautionary hygiene measure) I stepped into the bath, turned the rusty tap and let the familiar lukewarm water flow over my body. I began to sing thoughtlessly, as I often did when I showered, making up the words as I went along, 'Ba ba Bologna ooh ooh...A city so bella la la la la...' Then I felt a strange sensation on my head. At first I thought it was just the water which had a tendency to fluctuate in pressure, but slowly reaching up, my hand met something damp and furry. I let out a girlish scream which probably woke up the whole hostel and shook my head violently before jumping out of the shower and running into the corridor soaking wet, covered in soap suds and naked as the day I was born.

It just so happened that Roberto had chosen that precise moment to come and clean the bathroom. I forgot I was still wearing the plastic bags on my feet and slipped gracelessly onto the tiled floor, falling face first. Time seemed to freeze as we stared blankly at each other. I quickly got to my feet. Roberto's mouth gaped open slightly and he looked bleary eyed and utterly dumbfounded. I crossed my arms over my chest and managed to mutter, 'Giovanni's in the bathroom' before I hastily waddled back to my room, squelching as I went.

After that I knew I had to use any means possible to leave Amici hostel. That is, if I didn't want to become clinically insane, catch some sort of rodent-borne disease or die of embarrassment.

The following night at Piazza Verdi I was explaining my predicament to the others.

'You should check out Facebook' suggested Anita. 'There's a really good group called *'Affitasi Studenti Bologna.'*

'Aren't those accommodation groups full of weirdos and scammers though?' I asked, raising an eyebrow.

She took a drag of a spliff and blew the smoke upwards into the balmy evening before handing it to me,

'Well that's how me and Tatiana found our place' she said.

Her pretty round face glowed in the moonlight as she tucked a stray strand of her slightly bobbed chestnut hair behind her ear. I admired how perfectly it framed her face in comparison to my own untameable auburn curls.

The Piazza was particularly lively that night. Looking beyond our own group I could see smiles, I could hear laughter. Happy faces seemed to blend perfectly with the green shades of the beer bottles and the yellow glow which emanated from the surrounding bars. If there was ever going to be a city where I could put a little faith in humankind, it was Bologna.

'Well I suppose I have nothing to lose' I admitted,

'As long as there aren't any rats in the shower I'm sure you'd be fine' said Marc.

He smiled and looked straight into my eyes. I smiled back, blushing.

'So, Ronan told you all then?' I asked nervously.

'Yes' they replied in unison.

Ronan happened to be working at The Emerald that night so I couldn't even give him a cursory glance. He'd sworn he wouldn't tell the others. Well at least I thought he had after he'd stopped crying with laughter. I didn't think I would be able to recover any of my pride after the rat-vomit story.

'You're a bloody disaster K-dog but you're hilarious' boomed Edward, before shrugging his shoulders and letting a loud yawn escape.

Anita laughed and glanced over at him, her head slightly titled to one side.

Marc smiled slightly again and looked down as he picked away at the label of his beer bottle. An awkward silence hung in the air.

'Ah thanks, I suppose' I said, trying to hide my embarrassment and unsure about whether I was being complimented or mocked.

'Don't worry Kerry I'm sure you'll find something' said Tatiana in her soft husky voice as she reassuringly put a hand on my leg.

I could tell she was sincere but it was obvious she was also repressing a giggle.

'Thanks' I said, although I still wasn't sure if gratitude was the right sentiment.

'Well here's to falling flat on your face but getting up again' said Anita with gusto, raising her bottle to the centre.

'And always exposing the naked truth' added Edward raising his own bottle and sniggering,

'And no more rats' said Tatiana triumphantly.

'And fucking up with style' said Marc, his beautiful eyes sparkling in the half light.

'And friends like you' I added finally, raising my beer to the centre and smiling widely.

Our bottles clinked together in a harmonious chime.

Chapter 4

By the time my first day at the university arrived I was still home hunting. I had however taken Anita's advice and posted an ad to the Facebook page she'd told me about,

'20 year old female Irish student (because everyone loves the Irish) *desperately* (a hyperbole which albeit true was a sign that I was becoming more Italian by the day) *seeking room to rent in the centre of Bologna. Duration - 11 months. Clean, friendly and reliable. Non-smoker* (Nearly every Italian smoked like a chimney so that wasn't really an issue but I put it in for good measure.)'

I wrote it in both English and Italian hoping that either some *Bolognesi* or other Erasmus students would take pity on me and respond. Every day I spent at the Amici was now making me feel as though I was sinking deeper and deeper into the depths of Dante's inferno.

Whatsmore it was becoming increasingly difficult to avoid Roberto. I hadn't spoken to him since the rat-shower incident and wanted to keep it that way.

Still, I was excited about my first day of lessons. The Universitá di Bologna was after all the oldest university in the world and I felt truly privileged to be able to study there. Perhaps I could absorb the knowledge and wisdom of the countless other great minds such as Thomas Beckett and Copernicus who had philosophised and debated within those very same walls.

Maybe just being there would open my mind, inspire me to strive for success and unlock my full potential, letting nothing hold me back...not even rats called Giovanni.

Stepping into the main entrance atrium of the University of Bologna is a bit like stepping back in time. Not only are the weathered stone walls and columns ancient looking but covering the upper porticos are paintings of the family crests belonging to the first ever students from 1088 A.D. It really is stunning and I truly felt as though I was entering somewhere of monumental importance.

Once I'd taken a moment to get over the magnificence of the building itself I brought myself back to the present and found my way to the reception where I was given a list of all of the lectures on offer and a map of the campus.

'Sorry I think you've left out my timetable' I said to the impeccably dressed receptionist,

'Cosa?'

'You know , my *orario* so I know when to go to my lessons.'

The dark haired, typically gorgeous Italian woman just stared at me blankly and vaguely waved her perfectly manicured hand,

'Oh you do that *da sola.*'

'What, so I just choose which lessons I go to myself?'

'Si si, esatto.'

And with that she suddenly feigned interest in her computer screen, staring at it as though she was trying to send an e-mail using solely the power of her mind.

I walked away slightly confused. *Make up your own timetable? Who ever heard of such a thing? Only in Italy.* I skipped down some steps and slumped onto a bench in a little grassy quad to try and make sense of it all.

Ok so there is a lecture on French linguistics at 9am, I suppose I can go to that. Wait, but then there's one on Italian dialect at 9.30am which I suppose is more important but I'll miss most of that if I go to the other one. Oh, but then there's also one on Dante's inferno at the same time. God this is hopeless.

In the end I spent the day running around like a headless chicken, trying to sample as many lectures as possible so as I could make an informed decision as to which modules I wanted to continue. This just meant that most of my fellow students thought I was mad since I entered every lecture theatre panting, red-faced and flustered.

In the end it probably didn't really matter which classes I went to. I couldn't understand much of what was being said anyway. Nearly all of my lecturers were balding, slightly podgy Italian men with glasses who spoke faster than the speed of sound and gesticulated wildly whilst pointing at pictures and diagrams which didn't seem to bear any relevance to what they were talking about. I mostly just ended up staring at the amazing frescoes on the ceilings depicting biblical scenes and praying to God that my earlier theory about absorbing age-old intellect was right.

By the afternoon when it was time to leave I felt more than a little deflated. Then I remembered that I had to go back to the slovenly dwelling that was Amici hostel and suddenly I was a full blown puncture in need of repair.

As soon as I got back I immediately fired up my laptop so I could make use of the last hour of free wifi and check if anyone had responded to my ad. To my delight I had a message waiting.

Buon giorno Kerry,

I may be able to help your situation. I have a small apartment with two bedrooms and a kitchen. The Signora who owns the place told me I can sub-let the other bedroom so we could agree a price between us. I be to Ireland many times so I would love to meet you! Let me know if this is pleasing to you,

Saluti

Barbara

I was so happy I thought I could burst and couldn't help letting out a small squeal which must have been loud as I garnered a queer look from my normally inanimate Japanese roommate. I wasted no time in replying, my fingers joyfully attacking the keys.

The following afternoon as I made my way to the address which Barbara had provided I noticed that I was veering further and further away from the centre and by the time I arrived at Via Massarenti I was actually outside the boundary of the old city wall.

Ah well, beggars can't be choosers. This area of the city had a very suburban and unthreatening feel about it and as I passed little grocery shops and quaint bars, I began to quite easily picture myself living there. The apartment was almost at the very end of this lengthy street but when I finally arrived, I knew I was in the right place.

Barbara suddenly jumped out from behind a tall white gate as though she possessed psychic abilities and shouted '*Kerry, piacere!*' whilst assaulting me with the traditional Italian greeting of an air kiss on each cheek.

She was very buxom and I felt as though she was going to topple me over as she affectionately squeezed my shoulders. When she stepped back I could see she had a spiky blond hair cut which was perhaps a bit too young for her (I guessed she was nearing fifty) but seemed to perfectly compliment her cheeky grin and bright hazel eyes. I let her lead the way as she first showed me a little outdoor patio with some potted plants and cast-iron furniture.

'This would be perfect for a little party. You could invite your friends, have a few birra' she stated matter of factly as if she was in no way making a cringey effort to be modern or progressive.

I just nodded and smiled, still slightly winded from the initial greeting. Then we headed inside where I was shown the kitchen, adjoining dining room, Barbara's room (which also doubled as a living room) and the room which would be mine. This was the one I was most interested in.

Compared to my dorm at the Amici it was pure luxury. I don't think I'd ever seen a bed so big – it practically took up the whole width of the room. The rest of it was filled with ample wardrobe space and a dresser with a pastel blue colour scheme tying everything together in a homely ribbon.

From that moment on Barbara could have told me that she was ex-mafia, that the bed was a stolen asset or even that she'd once killed a man in it but I wouldn't have cared. I knew then and there that I wanted to live in that apartment. I noticed that Barbara was looking at me expectantly, trying to read my facial expression which was somewhere between awe and gleeful rumination.

'It's beautiful' I said, 'the colours and everything.'

'Ah yes this is the blue room' she said, smiling excitedly.

I stared at her blankly, thinking that such a statement was sort of unnecessary and obvious. I mean, I could see that it was blue. I wasn't colour-blind. Sensing my confusion she pointed out that she had systematically colour-coded each room,

'You see the kitchen is green, my room is red and this one is blue!' she explained, and she didn't just mean the colour of the walls. In each room everything from the curtains to the ornaments were colour co-ordinated right down to the skirting boards.

'Ahh capisco' I said, as though this was perfectly normal whilst smiling forcibly to hide my creeping suspicions that Barbara was a little crazy. This was something which I continued to do however as she proceeded to show me around the apartment. In the dining room there was a full-length film poster of Harry Potter and the Philosopher's stone and on the fridge there was another one with Bella and Edward from Twilight.

Maybe Barbara is a teenage girl trapped in an older woman's body I thought. Then I had the much more sensible initiative to ask,

'Ah do you have children?' whilst motioning to the posters.

'No, I just love Harry Potter and Twilight' she said, still smiling enthusiastically and nodding like a bobble head doll as she showed me the full sets of dvds and books pertaining to each franchise which lined the shelves of the small entrance hall. I continued to smile mechanically.

Then I noticed that Barbara's room, 'the red one' was completely covered in London related paraphernalia. She had a poster of a big red bus, a photograph of big ben, a clock in the shape of an underground sign and even a little model of a red telephone box perched on the mantelpiece.

'So, you must really like London then' I said.

'Oh siiiiii' she said, increasing in pitch and bouncing slightly as she led me into the room.

'I've been many times. I also lived there for six months but I couldn't find a job. You know with the *La crisis* it's hard.'

And for a second her face fell slightly, momentarily offering me a glimpse into the saddest recesses of her soul. Then she lit up again, seemingly abandoning all thoughts of economic recession as she firmly pulled me down on to the spongy sofa next to her,

'But I've also been to Ireland too. Many times. *Guarda!*'

And with that she pulled out an iPad, showed me some holiday photos and spent the next half hour prattling on about her visit to the Blarney stone, her nights out in Dublin, the time she camped in Connemara, all without taking a breath. I could barely get a word in edgeways and instead nodded sporadically whilst concentrating all of my mental efforts on just understanding what she had said in Italian. In the end, when she had to take a breath, I managed to ask the essential questions which I had come there for, like the cost of the rent, the deposit, utilities etc.

After that we chatted for a bit longer. Well Barbara chatted and I listened, before I realised that I'd been there for over an hour and made my excuses to leave. Then I noticed that Barbara's bedroom/living room didn't actually have a bed.

'Wait, where do you sleep?' I asked.

'Oh this is a sofa bed. Every night I just pull a sheet over it and add a few pillows.'

I couldn't possibly fathom why anyone would rather sleep on a camp bed when there was a huge bed which could comfortably accommodate three Barbaras in the adjoining room.

'Oh but you don't need to do that for me' I said, suddenly feeling humbled by what I assumed to be a kind act of sacrifice.

'I could sleep here and you can still have the big bed.'

'No, no, *tranquilla*, I have always slept here. I like being able to fall asleep in front of the *tele*.'

She made it seem like such a rational argument that I left it at that.

'Well, *ci vediamo*' I said after I assured her that I definitely wanted to take the room and scribbled down my mobile number.

She grinned and gave me a rib crushing hug as though this was her form of a legally binding contract.

'*Si si, ci vediamo*' she chirped, still beaming at me.

And with that I left feeling somewhat confused, a little bit disturbed but ultimately utterly elated that I now had a one-way ticket out of Amici hostel. That heavenly blue room was in my sights and there would be no turning back – not for anything.

Chapter 5

Bicycles in Bologna are like chewing gum in any other city. They're ubiquitous, disposable, fleeting, cheap and offered by looky looky men. It's also possible for them to leave an ugly mark on the pavement since I once saw a bike that had been rammed so hard by a car it had become welded to the kerb.

Incidentally the first bike I had in Bologna I technically stole. Well, I prefer the term 'recycled.' Barbara pointed it out to me the first morning after I moved in.

'I say if you hang on to a bike for two months here you do good' she said as she busied herself in getting ready for work. She was a member of the *Polizia Municipale* which is the Italian equivalent of a community police force. Somehow, I couldn't quite picture Barbara reprimanding someone and instead imagined her as some sort of comedy villain who spent her days chasing down criminals in hilarious slapstick fashion.

'Really, but how much are they?' I asked as she zipped up her navy jacket and adjusted her white cap in the hallway mirror, hopelessly trying to tidy the errant spikes of blond hair which protruded from underneath.

'Ah you can get one for ten euros in Piazza Verdi from one of the *africani* I'd say, but you need a good lock, not like that cheap crap by the *cinesi*' she said, wagging a finger at me. By this she meant the little plastic locks made in China which can be easily cut through as opposed to the big, hulking metal chains.

'*A Punto*, I have a bike you could use!' she said suddenly, pointing at me and then firmly clapping her hands together.

'*Daverro*, really?'

I tried to sound enthusiastic but it was early and I was still a little bleary eyed. For the first time in weeks I'd relished a good night's sleep in a comfy bed, in a room by myself, blissfully undisturbed.

'Ah well it's not actually mine...well yes it's not' she confessed as her left hand waved limp circles in the air.

'Oh right, whose is it?' I said suppressing a yawn as I leant against the doorframe of the bathroom.

'Well, *chi lo sa*? it's been in the courtyard for ten months and no one has claimed it.'

Her mass of keys jangled as she scooped them up from the kitchen table and stuffed them into her handbag. I wondered why she needed so many.

'Ah right, how come it hasn't been stolen?' I asked, my interest suddenly peaked.

She just gave a non-committal shrug and thrust her palms out like Tweety bird.

'*Chi lo sa*? Have a look for yourself, it's just outside. I'll make you *Lasagna* later for dinner if you like, Mamma's own recipe!'

And with that she bolted out of the apartment, firmly slamming the front door shut as my mouth hung half open on the point of forming a reply.

I was deadly suspicious of a bike that had been a sitting duck in a city were bike theft was rife. *What was wrong with it?* It's like when you pick the cat that is free to a good home and it's clearly the most beautiful feline you've ever laid eyes on and then you take it home and several concerned inquiries about self-harm later, you realise it was the last one for a reason.

The bike's problem incidentally was more dog related, as in, the seat had been chewed away revealing the yellow foam within. Apart from that though, it wasn't too bad. I took it to a *bicicletteria* to get it some new tyres and a bit of oil here and there. The tall thin man in the shop (who stood and watched whilst a short fat man did all the work) regaled me with a concise history of the stolen relic I'd brought to his attention.

'Ah how interesting, what a surprise!' he said, carefully annunciating every syllable. As he bent down to inspect my bike I noticed he had a name tag fastened to his navy boiler suit which read 'Marco.'

'Sorry, *in italiano* please. I need to learn' I said a bit more sternly than I needed to.

I'd been getting anxious about improving my language skills though and in urgent need of practice. The more time I spent with Ronan and the others, the less I was getting.

Marco didn't profess his desire to practice English (like every other Italian) but I could see it in the two seconds his face became downcast before he launched into a passionate and heavily gesticulated account of my bike's origins,

'So this bike, bikes with this exact design' he said, fervently pointing at the red and turquoise stripes which adorned the white frame, 'were created by the city council and given out to students as free bikes, but...' he now had a visible glint in his eye as the story came to a crescendo '...they discontinued them about ten years ago. I haven't seen one since...until today.'

With that he gazed over at it as though he was looking at a ghost. Meanwhile the short fat man just rolled his eyes as he struggled with a spanner and what was quite a rusty bolt,

'So it's vintage then!' I chirped, seeing it now not as a bike I had stolen but a bike which had lost its way and was just waiting for me to find it; a bike with an elaborate back story of loss and woe.

'Yes, well you could say that' he said, sounding rather unconvinced as he ran a hand through his wild curly black hair.

'So where did you get it?' he asked, raising an eyebrow.

'Ah, I found it, well my landlady found it first, she said it had been abandoned in our courtyard and that I could take it.'

'So, you stole it?' he said, grinning wildly.

'Well, ah no...' My cheeks flushed with embarrassment.

Marco just put a reassuring hand on my shoulder and laughed,

'*Tranquilla*, don't worry, this is *Italia!*'

I nodded conspiratorially.

When Marco's short and fat counterpart had finished he rather unceremoniously plonked my forgotten treasure on the floor and gave the bell a satisfied ding.

'*Pronto*!' he grunted and then waved vaguely at Marco before rubbing his hands gleefully and disappearing into a back room.

'*Eccola*, all done' said Marco, tapping the handlebars lightly with all the satisfaction of someone who had actually worked towards the finished result.

'Grazie mille.'

I smiled warmly at him, savouring the prospect of authentic Italian bike rides, gliding through piazzas and under porticos with fresh bread in the basket and flowers in my hair.

I decided to heed Barbara's advice so when I settled up I also bought a thick chain which rattled around in the basket as I later rolled into Piazza Maggiore to meet the gang.

'Oi oi, what we got ere then love' Edward chimed in a fake cockney accent as he rubbed his hands together.

He was sitting with the others on the steps of San Petronio and leaning back, looking as nonchalant as ever with a beer in hand, fully revelling in the irreverence of the scene. Anita was perched next to him, leaning on his shoulder and giggling into his ear. I pretended not to hear him.

'Yeah nice wheels K- dog' said Ronan who jumped up to eagerly inspect it as I chained it to the nearest lamp post.

Tatiana was eating a crêpe and looking as serene as ever, her long legs spread out across the steps. She tilted her head back unleashing a cascade of caramel hair as she took another bite with her soft peach mouth and smoothly swallowed. Meanwhile Marc, ever aloof, was poised on the ground with one knee bent, gazing at the stars and puffing calmly on a cigarette. He barely noticed my arrival.

'So what's the plan for tonight guys' I asked as I sat down next to Tatiana. She offered me a bit of her crêpe but I politely refused on the grounds that any way I ate it would just seem unladylike and vulgar, plus I had to think of my figure.

'Well, I thought we could all head to the Lord Lister' said Edward, now thankfully speaking in his normal voice.

'They've got a 2-4-1 deal on cocktails if you have an Erasmus card.'

Everyone hummed their approval.

The Lord Lister was only a stone's throw away from Piazza Verdi on Via Zamboni so we strolled down at a leisurely pace. Anita and Edward were holding hands. I raised a questioning eyebrow at Ronan who just shrugged his shoulders and gave me a look which said, 'I don't know and I don't care.'

It seemed to be a sudden development and one which I couldn't quite fathom. Admittedly, I did find Edward attractive on the surface. He had the sort of face that wouldn't look out of place on a Calvin Klein billboard with perfectly coiffed brown hair and cheekbones you could slice ham on.

But anytime he opened his mouth I had to take a deep breath and resist the urge to strangle him. I glanced over at Marc who seemed to be in a deep reverie. With his white billowy shirt and elegant stride he could have been a character from a silent film; a troubled soul gliding through a black and white screen.

Once at the bar we took advantage of the cocktail offer and all got suitably drunk on mojitos before heading down to the small basement dancefloor. The music which thumped from the speakers was a weird mixture of nineties Brit pop and European chart hits.

As the mojitos began to take effect it was more difficult to discern between tracks and they all just seemed to blend into one another, creating a continuous buzz of music as we danced close together in the smoky room. The place was packed out, mostly with Erasmus students but there were also some local Italian guys who could be irritatingly forward in their advances. At one point I had to escape from the clutches of a particularly sleazy one who kept touching my bum and trying to grind up against me.

'Where you from?' he kept blurting in my ear, since he had obviously come with the intention of going home with a foreign student.

I grabbed Ronan by the arm as he passed me and spun him round, firmly introducing him as my boyfriend.

Ronan only gave me a slightly inquisitive look before putting his arm around me and politely telling my groper to *'Vaffanculo.'*,

'Thanks Ronan' I said, visibly relieved as the guy slinked off in search of his next victim.

'No bother' he said winking at me, with a brotherly arm still around my shoulders.

'I knew those improv classes would come in handy.'

With that he took my hand, gave me a twirl and led me over to the bar.

'Let's do shots' he said excitedly, his eyes sparkling. I knew it was a bad idea but I could never seem to say no to Ronan.

'Alright, I'll have a Vesuvius' I said, feeling brave.

After I'd downed it I realised why they'd named a mixture of whiskey and vodka after a volcano. Ronan opted for tequila which seemed tame in comparison.

'Christ what's got into you! You know I won't be able to pick you off the kitchen floor tonight' he jibed as he gave me a nudge, nearly knocking me off my barstool.

'Look Ronan that was one time. One time!' I said, trying to smile but struggling since my face was still contorted from the Vesuvius aftertaste.

One night I'd been out drinking with the others and hadn't quite managed to make it to my room. Ronan had discovered me passed out in the kitchen with a cockroach crawling on my face after coming back from a late shift at The Emerald. Thankfully Roberto hadn't seen me in that particular compromising position.

When I'd moved out he wasn't on reception so I was a little sad I'd missed the chance to say goodbye to him. Bidding farewell to the Amici had been a bittersweet experience really. I was happy to leave behind the dirt and the grime but as I stepped into the taxi and gave it one last backward glance I realised it would always hold a special place in my heart.

'How are things at the Amici anyway, do they miss me?' My speech was already a bit slurred and I had to shout to be heard over the music.

'If by 'they' you mean Roberto then yes. He's positively dying. Can't get over it. It's only been a day but he's been pining for ye like mad. A man on the edge I tell ye.' He clutched his hands to his chest melodramatically.

'You're such a dick' I said as I punched him in the shoulder a bit more forcefully than I meant to.

'Uch sure it's only a bit of persiflage' he said airily, slapping me hard on the back before rolling up the sleeves of his bright geometric patterned shirt. It was almost as if he was preparing for a physical battle.

'What the fuck is persiflage?' I said incredulously, suddenly realising that I was at the stage of drunk where I can get a bit sweary.

'Ah it's just a fancy word for banter' he replied cheerfully,

'I learnt it the other day from this D.H Lawrence novel I've been reading. Actually, maybe you should read it, it's called 'Women in love.'

He smirked and tilted his head in a way that would have been so irritating were it anyone else.

'I'm too drunk for fancy words Ronan' I said with mock seriousness as I slapped a hand on the smoothly polished surface of the bar.

'And I'm not in love' I added rather solemnly.

'I am going to miss seeing that beautiful face every morning though.'

I looked upwards as my mind drifted to thoughts of Roberto, dashingly handsome Roberto whose lips I'd fantasised about kissing more times than I could remember. Infatuation is what it is though; shallow and sadly unfulfilling.

'Ah well sure you'll just have to make do with my pretty face now won't ye' he said, batting his eyelashes and theatrically pouting his lips.

'Hmm, I suppose so.' I said, trying not to laugh at how ridiculous he looked.

The thought of kissing Ronan was inconceivable. Not because I didn't find him attractive. He had his quirky charms and he made me laugh but he was like the brother I'd never had. In any case he'd already told me that he had a girlfriend back in Dublin; a girl called Rosie who he confessed to missing every now and then after too many pints.

'You fancy two more shots?' he said with not enough inflection since he knew it was more of a statement than a question.

'Absolutely.'

After a few more than just two shots we wound our way back through the crowd to the others who were now firmly getting into the party spirit.

Tatiana was up dancing on one of the tables to Hips Don't Lie by Shakira and exposing her belly ring as she shimmied this way and that, causing her top to ride up her toned stomach. A circle of admirers were gathered below her, clapping their hands in time with the music.

Through the blur of bodies and colourful moving spotlights I could just about distinguish Anita who was now writhing against Edward, her lips almost touching his as she locked her arms tighter around his neck. I danced with Ronan who was a maverick in terms of style, spinning me around madly and lifting me up in a way that lacked any spatial awareness.

After a while I sat down to catch my breath. Sweat was dripping from my forehead, and my head felt dizzy from all the shots. I looked over and saw Marc leaning with his back to the bar, solemnly observing the madness around him. As he turned to leave, I followed him back up the stairs and out into the street where he sat down on the pavement to light up a cigarette.

'Hi' I said, putting my arm gingerly on his shoulder to steady myself as I sat next to him.

He slowly turned to look at me, his lips forming a faint smile as he silently offered me a cigarette. I politely declined. He sighed and gazed off into the middle distance. It was one of those moments when I desperately wanted to say something poignant and interesting but my drunk mind just couldn't seem to find the words. We sat there for a while. Not speaking; just listening to the muffled thump of music and the hum of chatter emanating from people spilling out onto the street.

'If I hear Bailando by Enrique Iglesias one more time I think I might go insane' Marc said gravely before pulling that downward smirk of disapproval that is so typically French and exhaling a short burst of smoke.

'Yeah, I suppose it can get a bit annoying after a while.' I said even though I had to stop myself from humming the chorus.

'So um, do you go out a lot in France?' I ventured, wondering if the nightlife where Marc was from was overwhelmingly more exciting in comparison to The Lord Lister.

He tapped some ash onto the cobbles before looking at me intently with his striking eyes.

'It's not really my thing' he said with more than a hint of apathy, 'but I like to get drunk so I always come out anyway. I'm from a little fishing village in Brittany – Brest. There's not really much to do there except drink and take drugs.'

'Ah it's the same where I'm from' I said casually, even though it wasn't strictly true. Whilst I had engaged in a few semi-wild nights, Ballycastle is more of a cosy drink in a pub, walk on the beach kind of place.

'I've heard the scenery's nice in Brittany though, lovely countryside' I added inanely.

'Hmm yes I suppose' he said with an air of coolness that made me feel slightly uncomfortable.

I twisted a curl around my finger as we fell into silence again. A few revellers walked past us, babbling noisily in Italian as they moved through amber pools of streetlight. My head felt heavy so I let it drop a little, finding it impossible to resist the urge to close my eyes...

'Kerry! Kerry! Wake up!' a loud voice in my ear brought me back to consciousness.

I opened my eyes with a jolt and realised that I'd been sleeping on Marc's shoulder. It hadn't been too long since he still seemed to be smoking the same cigarette but I sensed his irritation. Feeling embarrassed, I stood up too quickly only to find myself losing balance and falling backwards as my wedge-heeled sandals gave way beneath me.

Marc jumped up in time and caught me with a firm grip under my arms.

'I think I'd better take you home, where do you live?' he asked rather forcefully,

'Ah, um Via Mass-a-ren-ti' I said, focusing hard on each syllable.

'Ah ok, that's not far from me. I live on Via Azzura. Let's go.'

And with that he swiftly put one of my arms around his neck and held my waist with the other as we hobbled back towards Piazza Maggiore. As I looked up at his determinedly composed face I had the distinct feeling that he'd done this before, probably on a wild drug fuelled night in Brittany.

'Ah my bike' I said as I pointed in the vague direction of where I'd left it earlier.

'You're not fit to ride your bike' he said rather sternly.

I nodded shamefully in agreement.

'Do you think you could hang on to me if I rode it for you?' he asked in a slightly softer tone.

I nodded again but I wasn't quite sure.

After we'd got in position, we made a slow crawl home as the bike strained under the weight of two people. I've never ridden on the back of a motorcycle before but I imagine it to be a lot more thrilling and romantic. Instead of the rev of an engine and the swish of hair billowing in the wind, all I could hear was the creaking of rusty spokes and Marc's panting as he grew increasingly out of breath. Nevertheless, I felt strangely at ease with the absurd dreamlike intimacy of the situation. As I breathed in Marc's subtle musky aftershave and gripped his soft cotton shirt, the warm night air washed over my face, gradually sobering me up.

'Marc, if you want we can just walk for a bit?' I felt guilty since I could see he was painfully struggling under the physical exertion of pedalling and I didn't want him to hurt himself.

'Ah-oh-no-it's-ok' he managed to say between choked gasps. I could never quite fathom the limits of the male ego.

When we arrived at my place, I invited him in for a glass of water since his face had become flushed and beads of sweat were gathering about his temples. I turned the key and creaked open the front door.

The apartment was dark and eerily silent. I suddenly remembered that Barbara was out on a night patrol and wouldn't be back till morning. I fumbled for the switch whilst Marc stood close behind me, breathing warm air on my neck and just barely touching my shoulder like some ghostly presence. I involuntarily shivered. When I'd flicked on the light I found a little note by the phone from Barbara to say she'd left me some lasagna in the fridge. My stomach rumbled at the suggestion.

'Ah this is a really nice place' said Marc, sounding pleasantly surprised.

I noticed with smug delight that he was admiring my ginormous bed which was just about visible from the hallway.

'Yeah it's not bad' I said casually. As I ushered him into the kitchen, I found myself wondering what sort of apartment Marc lived in. I pictured either a drug den scattered with needles and cigarette butts or a solitary room at the top of a tall tower, piled high with books.

As I held out a glass of water, he seemed to be staring at me, transfixing me with those enchanting eyes. His lips parted slightly and I wondered if the endorphins had gone to his head. A nervous excitement took over me. I didn't really know Marc that well but that was part of the attraction. He was mysterious and dark and sexy and for some reason, right there and then he wanted me. I closed my eyes in anticipation of his lips touching mine. *Oh God he's going to kiss me! He's going to kiss me!*

'Ah… Kerry, why is there a poster of Mussolini in in your kitchen?'

'What?'

I turned around and realised that instead of gazing at me lustfully, Marc had in fact been staring in horror at a poster of the infamous Italian dictator.

And just like that, my fantasy bubble burst.

Chapter 6

I'm slightly ashamed to admit that after a few weeks of living in Italy the initial wave of excitement and enthusiasm had fully washed over me leaving a salty yet bittersweet taste in my mouth. I was homesick, but I couldn't say I wasn't enjoying myself. On the contrary I counted myself lucky to have made so many great friends, to be living in a country with such a rich and vibrant culture and to be studying at a world-renowned university. I just missed the little things like a proper cup of tea made with fresh milk, braving the cold and rain to go out with my uni friends to the clubs and pubs in Manchester and toast with peanut butter. For some reason, still unknown to me, peanut butter is very rare in Italy and is only available in select supermarkets in an expensive organic form.

I was contemplating such things as I cycled home one evening from a late lecture on French history. Normally I found the topic of the French revolution riveting but on this day I just felt utterly apathetic towards everything, towards existence itself, as though I was trapped in my own little bubble of solitude. I couldn't face going home at that moment. I knew Barbara would likely be cooking up something traditional and insisting that I tried it whilst she talked a mile a minute and bustled manically around our little kitchen.

Also, I still hadn't broached the whole Facism topic and it was now hard to enjoy my dinner with Mussolini's eyes burning into me. I just wasn't in the mood. I wanted peace and quiet and a little bit of space to reflect; some personal bubble me-time. I rode towards the centre, past the Due Torri, along any streets which took my fancy, and barely pedalled as I just let the gentle incline of the cobbles pull me further into my own private bliss.

Eventually I ended up in a little side street which was mostly dark apart from a soft light which glowed from a trattoria at the end. The place seemed inviting enough so I went in and got a table *per una persona*. Inside it was decked out with gingham tablecloths and generation after generation of family portraits which I supposed depicted the past and present owners. I ordered a pear and gorgonzola risotto and a small carafe of red wine since I felt in the mood for treating myself.

Now some people think that only loners and psychopaths would go to a restaurant by themselves and would rather spend an evening pulling out their own eyelashes. I on the other hand happen to find it quite an empowering experience. At that moment it provided me with the perfect amount of low-level chatter so I didn't feel so lonely but at the same time I could retain my anonymity and was in no way obliged to join in any conversation.

Beside me an old woman was also eating alone, slowly slurping a large bowl of soup as though it were a practiced ritual. Most young Italian girls are stunningly beautiful – all dark and beguiling, but this woman was a typical *Nonna* perhaps several times over, with sun spotted, leathery skin and a thick silver plait which hung down her hunched back. I wondered why she was alone. Maybe she was just like me and wanted a little space, perhaps an escape from a family of fourteen who relied on her cooking every night or maybe she was a widow, or worse, a spinster, with empty cupboards who sought the same low-level hum of people as I did in order to drown out the hollow sound of loneliness.

Once I'd finished my meal I realised that I could be looking at a mirror image of myself in fifty years time (provided I moved to Italy and somehow my genetic make-up changed). What if I kept giving into every little twinge of loneliness, forever wrapping myself in my bubble of solitude? In all likelihood I would become a crazy old cat lady who ate soup by herself and whom everyone avoided because she smelt of sardines. I was young and so was the night, so I resolved to not let my evening resemble that of an old fuddy-duddy.

Once I'd paid the bill I headed straight for Piazza Verdi on the off chance that I'd bump into someone I knew.

Guided by the soft glow of street lamps, the vivacious exclamations of Italians greeting one another, and the rumbling of mopeds, I soon arrived. The city was alive and so was I. A quick scan of the square told me that neither Ronan nor any of the usual gang were there but it was absolutely jam packed. People were sitting everywhere creating a human patchwork carpet whilst others stood milling around or leaning against the opera house which was just opposite. I really didn't want to go home just yet. I'd somehow been charged with a sudden nocturnal vitality like a cat that wakes up at night to go hunting. The moon was full, my eyes wide and alert. I decided to mingle. Afterall, you never know who you could meet unless you say hello.

I chained up my bike and prowled through the adolescent throng, eavesdropping on both Italian and English conversations, trying to stalk out potential companions for the evening. I somehow ended up introducing myself to three typically Aryan looking Germans; two guys and a girl. I'm not surprised I don't remember their names. They were just insignificant details and I knew I probably wouldn't see them again after that night.

Conversation was easy enough. My tongue had already been loosened by the wine I'd had in the restaurant and the guys were generous enough with their beer. I don't even remember much of what we talked but one thing which sticks very clearly in my mind is that the girl was explaining to me the difference between the two ways to say 'I love you' in German. '*Ich mag dich*' is more akin to 'I like you' and is more common whereas '*Ich lieb dich*' is much more intense and is only used between star struck lovers or hyperbolic romantics. Neither of them sounded very amorous to me (more like a hacking cough) but I just nodded and drank my beer (one of the guys bought me my own in the end) and marvelled at the sheer randomness of the situation.

After a while we all hit a bar. Then another, and another and another. And in every bar we took a shot....and another, and another, and another. I don't remember exactly where we went and after a while each bar just seemed to blend into the next as though we were passing through magical connecting portals, each one more blurry than the last. In one place I spotted a bottle of Bushmills whiskey and proudly proclaimed that I came from a town near where it's made. The barman immediately gave me a shot *alla casa* and a sly wink. I don't remember much after that other than a vague awareness of being in a basement-like room filled with the thrum of a live band.

I woke up the next morning in a strange white room. I was in a bed, lying down with a drip in my arm. My head was spinning and my back ached. It seemed I'd also lost control of my bladder functions at some point during the night since the sheets beneath me felt damp. On my wrist there was a little white plastic bracelet which said 'Kerri O' neel. Gran Bretagna.'

The light was blinding. I groaned. My mental faculties hadn't fully returned and perhaps I was still a little drunk because the next thing I did was rip the tube out of my arm and stumble towards the desk straight ahead. The doctors seemed a little surprised to see me and gave each other a quick 'is she *pazza*?' look.

'*Dov'è Piazza Maggiore*?' I asked groggily, since I wasn't entirely sure where I was.

I was pointed in the correct direction by the somewhat dazed staff and strode out of *Sant'Orsola* hospital, determined to find my way to the university and my first lecture of the day. Everything was still a bit hazy and my stomach ached a little but thankfully it was quite a hot day so the dress I was wearing soon dried out, making me presentable from the outside at least, even if my insides were churning. I made a brief stop for an espresso and a brioche before mechanically continuing in my quest of stupidity.

To this day I still don't know how I managed to sit through a whole day of lectures. I'm not sure how much information actually sank in but thankfully no one questioned my vacant gaze or seemed to want to sit far away from me due to the fact I smelt of pee. My drunken escapades from the night before stayed my own shameful secret.

Around lunchtime when I was finally sober I found a note in my bag detailing all of the vitamins and fluids I'd been pumped with and a receipt for treatment totalling sixty euros! I was stunned. Luckily, I'd made a swift escape and they had no way of tracing me to force me to pay up – for that I was thankful at least.

By the end of the day I still felt a little worse for wear but I managed to slump along in a zombie-like fashion towards Piazza Verdi to retrieve my bike. The only problem was it wasn't there. I thoroughly searched both the square and its neighbouring side streets but I couldn't see it anywhere. Then I noticed a bike with the exact same frame as mine chained to a lamppost directly opposite the spot where I'd left it. Gone was the dog chewed seat, having been replaced with a new shiny black saddle and a fancy silver bell adorned the handlebars but it was unmistakable. It was mine.

Well, it had been until one of the looky looky men saw an opportunity and decided to make it their own little profitable, up-styling project. Of course, my key didn't work in the new lock which had been fitted. I thought about leaving an angry note, demanding to have the bike returned to me, but my fighting spirit was overwhelmed by nausea so I just walked home and fell straight into bed where I lay motionlessly ruminating over my misdemeanours. The more I thought about my bike, the more I thought about the hefty medical bill which now seemed to be burning a hole in my pocket. I did learn something that day after all – you can't escape Karma.

Chapter 7

By the start of October the temperature in Bologna was beginning to drop slightly as the seasons gently shifted and the foliage in the parks turned crisp and brown. At night a subtle breeze tinged the air meaning less people sat out in Piazza Verdi, opting instead to grace the opera in their finest attire or take shelter in the surrounding bars. Everything was becoming a little more subdued, a little more calm. I was glad since after my night in hospital I'd decided it was time for me to dial down the partying, drink a bit less and study a bit more. However, in the spirit of youth and with the desire to make the most of the fleeting remnants of the summer, I convinced everyone to book onto an Erasmus day trip to Ravenna which comprised of a historical tour of the city and, most importantly, a beach party.

'Hey K-dog, so did you ever ask your doll about the poster of you-know-who?' asked Ronan in a hushed tone as he leant over and poked me from the seat behind on the coach.

I cringed at the memory of Marc making a hasty exit from my apartment as I profusely denied ownership of said poster. The way Ronan referred to it brought a smile to my lips though – this wasn't Voldemort we were talking about. Then again, I thought back to Barbara's Harry Potter poster and wondered if there were some fascist undertones in the tale of the boy wizard.

'Ah yeah, well I pointed to the poster and asked her if she was a fan of Mussolini...' I thought asking someone outright if they were a fascist would seem too accusatory.

'And what did she say?' he asked impatiently. Marc had overheard us and was now glancing over from the opposite aisle. When he caught me looking back at him he promptly lowered his eyes to his book, feigning disinterest.

'Well, she just sort of nodded and said yes' I confessed tentatively, calling to mind Barbara's manic grin and how I'd been at a total loss as to how to proceed with the conversation. I'd already had some late night hypothesising sessions with the gang in Piazza Verdi and had hoped there'd be a reasonable explanation, like she was a collector of vintage historical propaganda or was planning to make it into a dartboard.

'Jesus Christ! And what did you say?' he asked, pressing harder on my shoulder. I jolted forward as the coach was now trundling along at quite a speed. Aside from the rumble of the engine I could hear a cacophony of different European languages, all chattering in excited tones.

'Well, nothing really but it gets worse...'

'What? how?' The bright sun warmed my face as it shone in through the window and I could feel my sweaty legs starting to stick to the fake leather seats. I noticed Marc was now leaning closer to us so he could hear. I swallowed nervously.

'Well then she pointed out that she also has some ceramic busts of him on the wall in the kitchen and a book of all of his speeches which she reads every night before bed.'

Ronan's eyes widened as I hurriedly tripped over my words, barely taking a breath.

'She said her father was a big Mussolini supporter and so are two of her three sisters, whilst the other one (who she doesn't speak to anymore) is very far left. I didn't really know what to say so I just left it at that.'

I inhaled sharply.

For the first time I thought I'd managed to leave Ronan lost for words as for a second he seemed stunned into silence. Then he just gave a short laugh, patted my shoulder and slumped back into his seat.

'God K-dog, and I used to think *I* was unlucky.'

By the time we reached Ravenna it was midday and the sun was high in the sky. I immediately regretted my decision to wear denim shorts since I soon found that they chaffed uncomfortably when I walked. I'd also opted for a short-sleeved lilac blouse which tied at the navel, verging dangerously into the crop-top category. What had seemed like a daring fashion choice in the morning now just left me feeling hot and nervously self-conscious. I swung my camera around my neck in an attempt to modestly cover my thin line of visible midriff.

'Hey nice camera' said a familiar French accent as I fiddled with the lens cap. Marc seemed to have snuck up on me out of nowhere, casting a slight shadow over my shoulder.

'Um thanks.'

I flicked my hair to one side and tried to look cool as I slowly slipped on my sunglasses. When I turned to face him he seemed to have his usual air of nonchalance and an inquisitive look as though he wanted to conduct some kind of psychological study on me. I wondered what he thought of my dark revelations about Barbara.

'Promise you'll show me your pictures later?' he asked, motioning to the camera.

I couldn't quite put my finger on it but something seemed vaguely different about him, something in his voice which made him appear crisper and a little more in focus.

'Oui, bien sûr' I blurted, unsure as to why I'd suddenly decided to practice my French with him.

He replied with a wry smile before turning to join the others.

I'd decided to break away from the gang, promising to re-join them later at the beach since there was an option to follow an Italian speaking guide and I wanted to practice my language skills. I was also glad that I wouldn't have to listen to Edward's obnoxious rhetoric since he seemed to think that a degree in history made him a god. For most of the journey I'd been subjected to the noise of him spouting random facts about Ravenna with Anita and Tatiana periodically making 'mmm' sounds to convince him of their enrapture. I just couldn't take it anymore.

The tour started out in front of a dull, fairly uniform red-brick building adorned with an Italian flag. However, our guide Maria, a lean, tanned and dark-haired girl from Rome soon informed us that what looks like a normal secondary school was in fact founded by Benito Mussolini. *Humph, I wonder if this is where Barbara went to school* I thought as I looked up at its imposing wooden doors set in a white columned façade. A couple of teenagers were huddled on its steps, smoking cigarettes and adding to the graffiti which stained one of the columns. As she tightened her ponytail and raised her clear melodic voice, Maria went on to explain that an aerial view of the *Liceo Classico Dante Alghieri* spells out the letters 'BM', initially intended as a signal to passing planes that Ravenna was a fascist city. A hum of intrigue rippled through the group.

As we moved on, I shuffled towards the front so I'd be better positioned to hear what Maria was saying. Only the odd word was escaping my comprehension so I smiled to myself, pleased that my Italian was clearly improving. My first impressions of Ravenna as a city were favourable. Although it didn't have the character and delightful rough edges of Bologna it was still bursting with history and culture. You just had to look beyond the sanitised veneer.

Next we visited the church of San Giovanni Evangelista which is one of the oldest churches in Europe, dating back to 424 AD. With a tone of sadness and regret Maria told us that most of it had been destroyed by an American bomb during WWII which was initially intended for the train station.

A unanimous grumble pervaded the group. Inside, soft light streamed in from high-set windows to grace some of the original surviving mosaics which decorate the walls.

As I took time to study each one, I realised that despite their simple designs, of things like birds and olive trees, they were a lot more intricate than first meets the eye. For a moment I let myself become totally lost in the muted reds, greens and blues of the swirling tile patterns. Like most things in life, they only come into focus when you take a step back.

Moving on, we arrived in Piazza San Francesco; a small square in the centre of the city, flanked by a library and a rustic old church of the same name. Here Maria pointed out a small plaque which marks Lord Byron's former residence and then told us the story of his illicit romance with Countess Teresa of Ravenna. My favourite part of this tale was that in order to express their love for one another they had exchanged letters and even cuttings of their pubic hair. I tried to imagine what it must be like to lovingly shave one's muff fluff, without the pain of waxing or fear of resembling a porn star, and to then ardently present it to your sweetheart. *Roses are red, Violets are blue, my hair is curly and my pubes are too*. Maybe receiving some guy's pubes in the post was the 19th century equivalent of dick pics. From that day on I couldn't think of Lord Byron in the same way.

For lunch I queued in a quaint side street for a piadina; a typical delicacy of the region of Emilia-Romagna. It's best described as a sort of doughier pitta bread which is stuffed with whatever filling you like and then toasted. I opted for parma ham and gorgonzola which melted gloriously in my mouth.

From the other side of the square I could see that a wedding was about to take place in the church. The bride in her dress of resplendent white silk and taffeta was flanked by stunning bridesmaids and carrying a bouquet of white roses. She looked like she'd just stepped off a film set. I held up my camera and just managed to catch a shot of her as she swept inside.

Our final stop on the tour was the Basilica of San Vitale; the city's main cathedral. From the outside it wasn't much to look at but as we followed Maria and stepped inside there was a collective intake of breath. Above us were several domed ceilings decorated with exquisite frescoes and mosaics depicting angels and saints, plants and birds, gods and goddesses.

As I looked up I was held captivated by their vibrant shades of gold, turquoise and red and felt myself drowning in a sea of beauty and colour. I held up my camera somewhat sheepishly, knowing that a lens could never fully capture the immense splendour of a place like this.

The elegant byzantine arches and columns which surrounded the basilica towered overhead, leaving me feeling quite insubstantial. There was silence, save for the tap of heels on the tiled floor, the click of my camera and the odd hushed murmuring.

There aren't many moments in my life which I wish I could go back and relive but this is one of them. As I breathed in the scent of incense and savoured the ethereal atmosphere I felt at perfect peace with everything around me, as though the dappled light and colours, the curves and the cupolas, had all aligned themselves in that moment to form an awe-inspiring spectacle; a corner of heaven saved just for me.

With all of the necessary cultural activities ticked off it was time for us to head to the beach. On the way we stopped off at a supermarket to buy some cheap booze and a few snacks. I decided to just get one two euro bottle of red wine and share it out with the others so I wouldn't get too pissed. My goals for the night were simple. I was to have a good time, remember everything and under no circumstances end up in hospital. By the time we arrived at the beach the sun was just about setting, casting an orangey glow on the calm sea. I waved over at the others who were sitting on the sand. Anita was laughing and reclining with her head in Edward's lap and from the empty cans scattered by their feet it seemed they'd already gotten through half a dozen beers between them. Marc had a sage expression and was reading the same book he'd had on the bus, some text on existentialism, whilst Tatiana and Ronan were pointing to something on the horizon. I looked out to sea and could just about make out a little yacht which bobbed gently on the distant waves.

We sat on the beach for quite a while, chatting freely and drinking an appropriate amount of alcohol as the sun slowly dipped below the horizon. After a day of walking in a hot city I enjoyed the feeling of the sand between my toes and the taste of the fresh, salty breeze. At one point Anita and Tatiana decided to practice their handstands whilst Ronan and I judged. The more we drank, the more we were inclined to just shout 'ten out of ten!' upon every attempt before both girls tumbled to the sand, contorted and giggling. Marc was quiet as usual but in a relaxed self-assured way, as though he was pondering the meaning of life. I would have given anything to know what he was thinking.

By nightfall, music started to blast from the little beach bar and the place came alive with the sounds of the Spanish students dancing and singing along to Enrique Iglesias tracks.

'Oh God not this again' muttered Marc when Bailando came on. He ran a hand through his thick jet black hair and sighed as though he was above such frivolities.

'Uch come on' said Ronan, slapping him on the back and offering him another beer, 'let's go and dance.'

Before long we were all on our feet, moving to the beat and feeling the rhythm. Over at the bar I noticed Maria our tour guide. She had let her hair down and with every illusion of professionalism gone, was now standing on a stool and readying herself to climb onto some stealthy man's bare shoulders.

I noticed some other guys playing a game of beach volleyball and one of them kept looking in our direction distractedly. After scoring the winning point he casually ambled over.

'Hey guys, you coming for a midnight swim?' asked the lanky blond Swede, rubbing his hands together cheerfully. Edward's eyes narrowed.

Tatiana didn't respond verbally but rather hastily ripped off her clothes to reveal the black bikini she'd put on underneath. Anita followed suit and the sight of both of their lean, perfectly formed bodies left me feeling inadequate and self-conscious. Sometimes no amount of cheap wine can make you forget your body insecurities. The boys shrugged off the suggestion saying they didn't fancy it. Gingerly, I pulled off my shorts, feeling glad that I'd at least remembered to shave my bikini line. Then I realised that I hadn't put my bikini top on under my clothes. In my scatter-brained morning preparations I'd only remembered the bottom half. I tried to explain my predicament discretely to the girls. The Swede however overhead and in a loud emphatic voice exclaimed 'Oh don't you have a bra on? That'll do fine!'

Edward and Ronan laughed as they each chinked open another beer and Marc looked over at me, smiling, somewhat sympathetically I thought. I twisted around uncomfortably for a moment, looking at my toes, half hoping the sand would swallow me up.

'Oh come on' said Tatiana, pulling firmly at my wrist,

'Yeah it's not a big deal' added Anita who was standing casually with her hips apart and her hands behind her head like a swimwear model.

Oh fuck it, yes just fuck it Kerry, get it off and get in the fucking sea. I took a deep breath, another swig of wine and then pulled my blouse over my head, exposing my faded beige granny bra for all to see. Anita and Tatiana cheered and wooped their approval and each grabbed one of my hands as we raced uninhibited towards the water's edge, kicking up flurries of sand as we went.

Considering the hour and the time of year, the water was surprisingly tepid and I dived into its black velvet folds, guided by a slither of moonlight which rippled on the surface. From underwater, I could just about hear the girls' laughter but it seemed muffled and far away. I swam on, enjoying the sensation of being weightless and free, no longer worried about my body hang-ups. There's something magical about going for a swim at night, as though the allure of exploring a watery kingdom is all the more mysterious and enticing under the cover of darkness. As I looked up to the marbled surface of the water I wondered what it must be like to be a fish or a dolphin and live your whole life with the constant support of an intangible force. By the time I came up for air I realised that I'd swum quite a bit out and began a hasty breaststroke, splashing my way back to shore. When I reached the shallows Anita was floating on her back, gazing up at the starry sky whilst Tatiana, in record time, was in up to her waist and passionately kissing the Swede. I regressed to my schooldays as I waded past them childishly singing 'love is in the air, do-do-do, do-do-do.'

Tatiana just smirked at me and gave a cute laugh, splashing a bit of water my way. The Swede grinned unashamedly, tightening his grip on her slim waist and running a hand through her hair.

When I got back to where we'd been sitting on the beach, I found Ronan on his own since Edward and Marc had gone to the bar. I shook myself off a bit, like a dog, since I'd forgotten to pack a towel and then hurriedly pulled my blouse back on before I joined him on the sand.

'Good swim?' he asked.

'Yeah it was thanks' I said, suddenly noticing that my wet bra was seeping through, leaving two damp patches.

'Tatiana's getting lucky' I said happily.

'It must be the sea air.'

'Well I'll drink to that' said Ronan, raising a beer.

I noticed he had a few freckles on his cheeks now, most likely brought out by the sun.

'Yeah me too' I added as I clinked my wine to his beer and took a gulp straight from the bottle.

'So why don't you tell him that you like him?' he said suddenly. I stared at him blankly for a moment feeling quite confused.

'Who?' I thought maybe he'd mistaken my comment about Tatiana for jealousy.

'Marc' he said matter-of-factly. I felt a sudden surge of panic.

'What? No, no, no, no. I don't like him. Well, we're just friends.'

'Oh come on Kerry, you're always staring at him.'

'What no I'm not!' *Am I?*

'Yes you are.'

Is it that obvious?

'Well only sometimes.'

But it doesn't mean I fancy him

'You're doing it now!' he exclaimed.

At that moment I realised that I was in fact looking over to where Marc was standing. He was doing his usual nonplussed pose, leaning backwards on the bar and resting on his elbows, managing to look both incongruous yet incredibly cool. I had to admit that I felt something, some bubbling rush of attraction deep in my stomach, even if I wasn't entirely sure why - even if it scared me half to death.

'Ok, I fancy him, so what?' I said defensively, feeling somewhat vulnerable now that my secret had been exposed.

'So, you have to tell him' he urged enthusiastically.

I gulped. The thought of telling Marc that I had any sort of romantic feelings towards him was a terrifying one indeed.

'No, there's no way I could do that' I said firmly, taking another sip of my wine.

Of all the many scary things in life, I still maintain that telling someone how you truly feel about them requires the most courage, a leap of blind and reckless faith. My feelings were safely stowed away in a box which was usually kept tightly shut. I wanted to keep it that way. But Ronan wouldn't let it go. He teased me relentlessly about it, even when I tried to move the conversation onto different topics like the weather or Lord Byron's pubes.

'Ok, you're right' I said eventually, feeling somewhat defeated, 'I'll go over right now and ask him out.'

With that I stood up and strode valiantly towards the bar as the warm night air enveloped me in a dream-like cocoon. My heartbeat quickened and I suddenly felt light and floaty as though I was having an out of body experience.

When I reached the threshold of the beach hut I turned back to see Ronan swigging the last dregs of his beer and giving me the thumbs up. I smiled weakly in return and gave a little nod of assent as though I was embarking on a secret mission. Moving forwards, I could see Marc was standing in the same place as before, with the same air of ennui as the twinkling fairy lights overhead cast a soft glow over his face. *Target acquired, commencing phase 1.*

He noticed me coming towards him before I had a chance to figure out exactly what 'phase 1' was.

'Oh hi' he said breezily. 'Did you have a good swim?'

He smirked and I realised his eyes had fallen on the two wet boob patches on my blouse. I cringed as I subtly tried to cover them with my still damp hair. I anxiously ran my hands through it in an attempt to tease out the tats.

'Ah, yeah it was thanks. Very um…wet.'

I tried to grip the bar but my palms had become sweaty so my hand slipped causing me to stumble a little. Flirting had never been my forte. Marc raised an eyebrow, probably thinking I was drunker than I actually was. *Ok, phase 1 here we go.*

'So I was wondering if um…well I thought that…well it was just an idea since you're French, you know, a native speaker and I study French as part of my course.' His eyes widened slightly with intrigue as I rambled on, struggling to get to the point,

'Well, I just thought that maybe we could do a tandem exchange sometime? You know go for a drink or something, talk in French for a bit, English for a bit.'

I realised I'd been involuntarily chewing the inside of my cheek and promptly stopped. Marc licked his lips as though he needed a second to mull it over before leaning over and gently squeezing the top of my arm,

'Yes, why not, it should be fun' he said with a most uncharacteristic wink. Between this, the unexpected physical contact and the fact that he'd actually said yes to my proposal, I wasn't sure what surprised me the most. Despite feeling almost nauseous with excitement I breathed a sigh of relief and smiled somewhat cunningly. It was the perfect ruse. We'd go out somewhere, it would look like a date, feel like a date but as far as Marc knew it was nothing more than mutually beneficial language practice which with any luck would lead to further mutually beneficial arrangements. As I looked once more into Marc's eyes the thump of Europop muffled my inner critic, dampening the fear that a guy like him could never like a girl like me.

Target attained – phase 1 complete.

Chapter 8

A week later I was sitting in The Emerald, slowly sipping a whiskey on the rocks and desperately trying to calm my nerves before my 'date' with Marc. It had been Ronan's idea.

'Sure swing by the pub while I'm working and I'll give you a wee pep talk' he'd said.

However, it was an extremely busy Saturday night which meant that he'd barely had a chance to say hello to me before his services were required at the other end of the bar by a gaggle of eager punters. Among them was Signora Ricci, a fifty-something widow who wore fur, heavy gold earrings and a devilish rouge-lipped smile. She usually dropped by at least once a week for a Campari and generously tipped Ronan for his shameless flirtations. '*Che Bellooo*' she would coo with a rasping voice as she stroked the side of his face with a scarlet fingernail.

Mario, the short and stout owner, eyed me suspiciously as I sat down. He hated it when Ronan's friends visited since we usually distracted him, leading Mario to roll his eyes and break up our conversations with a clap of the hands and a brusque yell of '*Basta!*' Ronan being Ronan would just laugh, give us a cheeky wink and at some point of the night when Mario's back was turned, he'd slip us a free drink.

For now though all I could do was sit quietly with my own thoughts and look at the familiar décor which consisted of faded green leather seat coverings, an old broken fiddle and black and white pictures of iconic landmarks such as the Cliffs of Moher.

'Hey, are you Kerry?'

An American accent cut through the soft melody of Breathless by The Corrs which was playing behind the bar. It seemed Mario only had three CDs- The Best of The Corrs, a U2 singles album and the soundtrack to Riverdance. I swivelled round on my stool to face a tall, dark and rather smart-looking guy who was smiling at me as though he'd just bumped into an old friend. It was rather unnerving.

'Ah...yes that's me' I said tentatively before taking another sip of whiskey.

'Do I know you?'

I knew I wouldn't have forgotten him if I had. He was the first person I'd spoken to other than my lecturers to wear a shirt and tie, not to mention the fact that he was extremely attractive. The cogs turned wildly in my mind. He leant back a little, still smiling amusedly as though we shared some kind of inside joke.

'Oh, you probably don't remember but a few weeks ago I was out with my roommates and...'

Suddenly it clicked.

'...and you rang me an ambulance! Oh my God, thank you so much!' I involuntarily grabbed him by the shoulder as I felt a rush of embarrassment, surprise and wonder all at once. He gave a short laugh, and shrugged as though it meant nothing, as though he rescued incapacitated drunk girls all the time.

'Yeah don't mention it. I'm just glad you're ok.'

He undid the top button on his shirt, loosening his tie a little before wiping away a few beads of sweat which had formed under his collar.

'Yes, God knows what would have happened if you hadn't of... Thank you so much! Please, please let me buy you a drink to say thanks.'

As I spoke I made emphatic hand gestures and my voice rose slightly in pitch. This caught the attention of Ronan who gave me a quick look as if to say, 'What are you on?' as he topped up Signora Ricci's glass. He was probably intrigued by the fact that I was talking to a stranger since usually if I came to The Emerald on my own I would just be engrossed in a book, trying my best to avoid eye contact with Mario.

The American waved his hand and shook his head slightly in the same way I often do when my mum's trying to offer me another cup of tea.

'So um, what exactly happened?' I asked with some trepidation, gripping my glass tightly as though to brace myself against the flood of potentially mortifying details.

'Well, yeah, so I was out with my buddies and we ended up in Café Paris. You know that little place on Via Petroni?' I didn't really but I nodded anyway.

'Yeah well there was a band playing and when we arrived you were sitting on the bar just enjoying the music...'

He paused to look at me and I could tell he was considering whether it would be kinder to tell a modified version of the truth. I wondered what had become of the Germans and figured that they'd probably just ditched me when I got too drunk. They seemed to be the types who knew their limits.

'And then?' I asked nervously.

'Well then you were making out with this guy. I mean really going for it. He left when you started trying to unbutton his shirt. I think he was German.' *Oh scheisse.* Well that explains it.

'Then you climbed on to one of the tables and were dancing there for a bit. Then the next time I looked you were on the floor for but you were still conscious and able to prop yourself up on your elbows so I thought you were just having a rest.'

Oh God. I cringed at the image of people becoming increasingly irritated as they had to step over me.

'Oh Jesus, that's so embarrassing. Does it get any worse?' I already knew the answer.

'Look, hey if you'd rather not know I don't have to tell you but it's really not that bad. I'm sure you're not the only one.'

He put his hand on mine as though to reassure me that I wasn't the most tragic person to ever walk the planet. I tried to imagine all of the possible scenarios and thought back to the damp dress I'd woken up in the next morning.

'Oh my God, did I piss myself in the bar?'

I put my face in my hands, all dignity now lost.

'Ah... no you didn't' he said as he rubbed his stubble and laughed again before wiping away a moustache of beer foam.

'Why would you think that?'

'Oh, ha-ha, no reason at all.'

Moving swiftly on.

'Um so, how come I needed an ambulance?'

'Yeah well, my buddies and I were just about to leave and we saw you sitting crouched down on the sidewalk. Your mascara was running so I think you might have been crying?'

It was entirely possible but I decided to look bemused as though I was never that girl who gets sad or depressed on a night out.

'Anyway I live with Italians and they kept asking you where you lived and what your name was but you were just sort of mumbling. It was only when I asked you in English that you said your name was Kerry, but when I asked you again where you lived all you kept saying was 'with Barbara and Mussolini.'

He raised a curious eyebrow and I smiled into my whiskey as I explained.

After that Barbara continued to form a large part of the conversation. I ranted on about her little quirks like the fact she'd once decided it was a reasonable idea to start drilling holes in the walls to put up some shelves at 4am. The American laughed and listened patiently to all of my stories, only occasionally looking at me like I was crazy. He had a warm, forgiving smile too – the kind that doctors sometimes have to put you at ease when you're rambling too much. When I finally let him speak I found out that he was a twenty-five year old English teacher from Chicago who played bass guitar and despite living in Italy for nearly two years, still thought deep-dish pizza was the best. That night was the first time he'd ever been to The Emerald.

'The daylight's fading slowly, but time with you is standing still...'

'Oh shit I have to go' I said suddenly. Breathless was playing again as I glanced up at the old mahogany clock above the bar and quickly jumped down from my stool.

'It was lovely to meet you and again, I really can't thank you enough' I said, hastily shaking his hand as though we'd just reached the end of a business meeting.

He regarded me curiously, smoothing down his tie as though searching for the right response. I was about to dash off before I turned around one last time.

'Oh I'm so sorry. I forget to even ask you your name?'

'It's James'

'I'm Kerry'

'I know'

'Ah yes. Well lovely to meet you. I'd love to stay and chat but I'm late'

And with that, before James could say another word, I was running out the door, jumping on my bike and rounding the corner onto Via del Pratello as fast as I possibly could.

By the time I reached Piazza Maggiore I was slightly flustered and out of breath. On weekends the main square and the whole length of Via dell'Indipendenza came alive with street performers from contortionists head-to-toe in blue body paint to magicians in sparkly suits. The place was teeming with people and I struggled to weave my way through the bustling crowds. I stopped for a moment, briefly captivated by fire dancers who matched their blazing trails of light to the throbbing rhythm of African drumming.

I realised I should have been more specific regarding the meeting place. Faces seemed to blend into each other as I searched for one I recognised. When I finally spotted Marc he was leaning against Neptune's fountain, puffing calmly on a cigarette. I called over to him but my voice was lost in the rambunctious multitude.

'Marc! Marc!'

It was hopeless. I tried waving to him as well. First with one arm and then with both as my frustration grew. This was a mistake however as I forgot I was still sitting on my bike. I lost my balance and flopped gracelessly to the ground with a loud clatter. A few passers-by hurriedly rushed to my aid.

'*Signorina, Signorina, tutto a posto*?' enquired a broad shouldered man with glitter in his beard.

I was a little bit in shock but nodded furiously and replied '*Si, si si*' since my only injury was a cut on my knee and I'd ripped an ugly hole in my tights. *Merda*. The man helped me to my feet and I thanked him before making a slow crawl over to Marc. He now had his back to me, facing Neptune's mottled green arse. I gave him a soft tap on the shoulder.

'*Bon soir, je suis vraiment désolée d'être en retard*' I said in my best French accent as he turned around to greet me. He smiled and a beam of moonlight illuminated one half of his face as we air-kissed in the French way; one on each cheek. Stepping back he noticed the rip in my tights and the crimson slither of blood which was now trickling down my leg.

'*Putain*! What happened to you Kerry?' he asked as he deposited his cigarette butt in the fountain's murky water. A mermaid at its base gripped her naked breasts, fixing him with a cold marble glare.

'Oh, haha it's nothing, *rien de rien*. I just fell off my bike.' I tapped the saddle as though the bike itself was somehow at fault.

'Ah, *comment*? Were you going too fast?' he asked softly, taking another step closer.

I didn't want to admit that I'd managed to fall off my bike from an entirely stationary position so instead I confessed to being a bit of a daredevil. Marc laughed and told me off in a mock serious tone, urging me to be more careful as he lightly touched the crook of my arm. I promised I would. Once I'd locked up my bike we crossed the Piazza and stepped under an archway onto a quaint side street which hummed with the clinking of glasses. After choosing a table on a terrace we both ordered a beer.

'So where did you get your new bike from anyway?' Marc asked as he slowly crushed a peanut between his finger and thumb.

'Ah well it's a funny story really. I bought it off a priest!' It was true. I'd been looking for the Modern Art museum when I asked a man in Piazza Maggiore for directions. We chatted for a while and I ended up explaining to him how annoying it was that it took me twice as long to get anywhere since my bike had been stolen. His thin drawn face instantly lit up and he urged me to follow him round the back of San Petronio Cathedral where he had a couple of bikes chained up.

He offered me a beautiful specimen with a sleek black frame embellished with silver flowers for only twenty euros. I was overjoyed. He even pumped up the tyres and gave it a bit of oil before sending me on my way. It was only as I was thanking him and asked his name that I realised he was a priest.

'Sono Padre Vincenzo Fabbri' he'd said proudly as he bowed and kissed my hand, not neglecting to say that if I ever needed him he'd be in the sacristy of the cathedral, watching Formula one.

Marc smirked, fixing me with his wide, searching eyes as I relayed the story. When I'd finished all he said was '*Eh bon*, Kerry. What an interesting life you lead' before flicking a peanut into the air and throwing his head back to catch it in his mouth. I wasn't sure whether he was being sarcastic or not.

The night air was tepid and the tension palpable as I felt increasingly uneasy in my own skin. Since we were sitting outside I was aware of the eyes of passers-by, glancing at as, smiling warmly with the assumption we were a couple. A man selling roses veered dangerously close to our table but was diverted by a well-dressed man who stopped to buy one for the glamorous woman on his arm.

I gulped down my beer quickly and wasted no time in ordering another.

'*Est-ce tu veux un autre*?' I asked.

'No, I'm fine thanks' he said. I realised he still had half a pint left. *Shit, I'd better go easy, don't want to end up steaming.*

I hastily lined my stomach with a handful of peanuts.

'So, *Est-ce que tu as des frères ou des soeurs*?' *God, I sound like a GCSE French Oral examiner.*

'No I'm an only child, you?'

'Me too!' I sparkled with the hope that this was the first of many things we would have in common, a gateway to realising that we were in fact soulmates.

'Yes, I don't think my parents felt like having more children after my father's affair' he said blankly.

Well, I don't think I'm in the realm of GCSE vocabulary anymore.

'Oh, ah, Marc, I'm sorry that must have been horrible.' I stuttered awkwardly as I gripped the cool surface of my glass.

'Oh, don't worry, it made life a bit more exciting when I found out he was fucking his secretary' he said plainly, rocking back nonchalantly in his chair.

'Shit, I'm sorry' I blurted, as though I was personally responsible. *A liaison with the secrétaire. Quel cliché.*

I was now on my third beer, feeling the fuzziness rise to my head and saw this as my queue to divulge something personal in return, as though we were playing a game of trauma tennis. I gulped and nervously twiddled a strand of hair.

'My parents are divorced as well. But there wasn't an affair. I suppose they just stopped loving each other at some point.'

I half smiled with a vague sense of sadness. My parents never really talked about their split. It had happened when I was about five so I didn't remember it but I'd seen the photo of them on their wedding day – Mum with her pearly white smile and mega-perm, dad with his wonky bow-tie. I'd often wondered how a love that had once shone so bright could one day turn so sour. A picture tells a thousand words, but I suppose no-one ever said they had to be true.

'Oh my parents didn't divorce' said Marc emphatically as he flicked a small peanut morsel off the table.

I stared blankly in confusion.

'No, really, my mother acts like it never even happened. *C'est bizarre.* After months of broken plates, shouting and screaming, it all went quiet and she just acted like nothing was wrong. Six years later and I think she'd still rather stay married to a lying piece of shit than be on her own.'

His jaw clenched as he shook his head. It was probably the most emotion he'd ever shown and despite the awkwardness I felt, it was almost a relief to see that he was human.

I didn't know what to say so I just sat there in silence. Time seemed to slow down as we just looked at each other; Marc with a fiery glint of resentment in his eyes, and me with a drunken, glazed over expression.

'Ah, well, um, do you have a favourite film?'

In my drunken mind I had seamlessly changed the subject but in reality Marc just raised an eyebrow and laughed at me before replying 'no, I don't really watch films.'

Still, this opened up the conversation again and we spoke for a while longer about mundane things, leaving family dramas to one side. I realised that I'd never even asked him what he was studying. When I found out it was philosophy I can't say I was surprised.

'So, what's the meaning of life then?' I asked with a stupid grin on my face. I'd now moved on to red wine and could just about speak without slurring my words.

'*Bah, je ne sais pas.* I don't think there is one Kerry. I suppose we're all just trying to get through it, one way or another' he said as he gazed into the bottom of his empty glass.

'Hmmm, yeah I suppose so.'

I shivered and drew my shawl more tightly around my shoulders as a cool breeze rushed past. We'd been there quite a while so the street was practically empty now. Most of the restaurants were closing up, and the buzz of people had been replaced by an eerie quiet.

Marc walked with me most of the way home as I slowly pushed my bike through the cobbled streets. We didn't talk but there was no void, just a comfortable silence. When we reached the point where our two streets intersected it was time to say *au revoir*. I gripped Marc's arm gently as we performed the usual French goodbye; one air kiss on each cheek. It was only for a brief moment that my lips lingered in front of his, poised on the edge of a Freudian slip.

'Well, that's it then. I suppose I'll see you soon...or...or anytime you want' he said.

He smiled coyly as he turned his back on me and walked away, one hand in his back pocket, jacket slung lazily over one shoulder.

As his footsteps faded I took a moment to gaze up at the sky. The stars were out that night, dressed in all their sparkling glory and when I closed my eyes I could still see them, filling my heart with the light of endless possibilities.

Chapter 9

Tentatively, I dipped a toe in the water. It was lukewarm and bubbles from the jet stream tickled my skin. Dance music thumped in my ears whilst squeals of laughter reverberated throughout the room. Everywhere I looked there were beautiful people with chiselled abs and smooth legs.

I'm not drunk enough for this.

As I adjusted my cat ears and fiddled with the straps of my swimsuit I felt a wet hand on my waist.

'Hey, why haven't you been in yet? You're still dry' said Anita.

Her hair was slicked back and a few water droplets clung to her chest. She looked like a Bond girl, elegantly poised with a cocktail in her other hand.

'Um, I'm going in now, where is Tatiana?'

'Ah, well she's in the sauna with Erik' she said with a knowing wink.

'That Swedish guy? Is that still a thing?' I was a little surprised since I hadn't heard her mention him since the beach party.

'Yeah, he's been round our apartment a few times, but I think they want to keep it a sort of secret.'

'Ah right, I see' I said.

But I didn't. It didn't seem like there was any need to be coy since everywhere I turned all I could see were fornicating couples; in the pool, in the jacuzzi. I dreaded to think what the water might be composed of.

The people in charge didn't seem to care either. They just stood there like stony faced centurions, only scolding when someone was running by the pool.

'So go on then kitty cat, don't make me push you in' she said with an impish smile as she poked me in the ribs.

I sighed and sat down on the hard edge before sliding in. This was definitely the most unconventional way I'd ever spent Halloween. We were at a swimming complex about an hour's drive away from Bologna for yet another Erasmus party.

'Hey where's Edward?' I said as I stood on my tiptoes to keep my head above water. I didn't really care but even the familiar face of an arsehole might have made me feel less self-conscious in that moment. It was a pity Ronan had to work a double shift. Marc just said, *'Ce n'est pas mon truc.'* It wasn't his thing.

'Ah yeah I'm going to look for him now' Anita replied. 'Have fun!' A slight frown wrinkled her forehead as she turned to walk back towards the bar. I could tell something wasn't right.

For a while I just clung to the edge of the pool, not wanting to become unsuspectingly entangled in some sort of aquatic threesome. Of all the experiences I'd envisaged before coming to Italy - the pinnacle of art and culture, a water orgy hadn't been on my list.

Fortunately, no one could see my flabby thighs now that I was safely submerged. With a flush of embarrassment, I realised that I was the only one who had opted for fancy dress and the only one in a full body swimsuit. The thought of wearing a bikini made me want to pull my eyelids off but now I stood out even more. I might as well have written 'I'M INSECURE' across my forehead.

I imagined what Ronan would do if he was there and pictured him dive-bombing into the pool, splashing water everywhere and laughing in the face of the stern guard who'd tell him off.

'Uch, sure ye only live once' he'd say.

Having swiftly made a decision to wise up and at least pretend I was enjoying myself, I moved into a cautious breaststroke. It was pleasant enough and I reached the opposite side of the pool unscathed, so I continued, navigating the human assault course as best I could.

Then, round about my twentieth width, I was accosted mid-stroke by a swarthy-skinned Spaniard who grabbed my wrist and pulled me into a slightly shallower alcove of the pool. It seemed to be the most popular spot for lovers as three other couples were locked in tight embraces, panting heavily and performing some of the best exhibitionist snogging I've ever seen.

He clutched my waist tightly with strong hands and gazed at me dreamily with a face that was attractive yet lacked vivacity, like a perfectly painted mannequin.

I was bemused and tried to talk to him but it was hard to hear my own voice above the noise of the party. Then he whispered into my ear 'Do you want to go somewhere?'

I felt a surge of panic. If I'd maybe had a few more mojitos I might have taken up his offer, but I was more or less completely sober and he was a drunken mess. Emphatically I said 'No' and tried to swim away but he grabbed my leg and pulled me back like a shark latching onto a joint of meat. Again, he whispered suggestively in my ear, 'Do you want to go somewhere?' and again, more forcefully this time, I told him 'No!'

For some reason he took this as his queue to kiss me, hard and almost violently like he was trying to devour my face. I winced at the taste of his mouth, the sharp and lingering tang of Sambuca. Every time I tried to swim away he pulled me back and the current was in his favour since a jet stream separated us from the rest of the pool. Then he slipped a hand underwater and groped clumsily at my inner thigh, fervently attempting to inch his fingers inside my swimsuit.

In a flurry of frustration and vague fear I slapped him hard, splashing chlorinated water into his eyes as I made my escape.

'*Joder*!', he cursed, as he rubbed his eyes vigorously, '*Qué puta...*'

I hastily hoisted myself out of the pool and flopped onto the tiles with a wet thud.

Pushing past the crowds, I scurried to the bathroom, relieved to shut the door on the wild thrum of high-pitched laughter and techno pop. I gripped the edges of the sink with clammy palms, steadying myself and closing my eyes as I breathed in two, three, four and out two, three, four. My head felt hot and my heart strained, punching my chest from the inside. It was the first time in a while that I'd had a panic attack, that sensation that the ground was opening beneath me with nothing there to break my fall.

I tried to think of calm, relaxing things – azure waters, kittens, a sunset, fields of lavender, fresh coffee. I don't know how many minutes passed but eventually I uncoiled and relaxed, as the adrenalin drained away like dirty bathwater. I reached up and wiped away some of the condensation on the mirror. I hadn't worn waterproof make up. When I looked up, my mascara and whiskers were smudged, running down my face in heavy black rivulets. I snorted at how ridiculous I looked. I'd been going for 'sex kitten' but instead had achieved 'drowned cat.' *Sterling effort Kerry.* I splashed my face with warm water and tried to scrub as best I could, but my cheeks still had a greyish tinge like I'd been down a slate mine.

Just as I was disposing of my soggy cat ears in a bin I heard a distinct moan. At first I thought I'd maybe just imagined it but then I heard it again, an 'ooahh' with a pitch somewhere between pleasure and pain, coming from the row of shower cubicles behind me. I was about to make a hasty retreat when I heard something else.

'Mmm you like that don't you' spoken in the clipped tones of a public school boy and the unmistakable squeaking of bodies grappling in a confined space. My heart sank. I could have just run out of there, feigning ignorance but my morbid curiosity got the better of me, so I turned around and peered inside the offending cubicle. It wasn't locked. All I had to do was gently pull the door towards me, revealing a naked Edward with a lithe red-head who had snaked her legs around his waist and was now screaming his name. I froze. My mouth hung open like a marionette, but he had his back to me and her eyes were screwed shut, too consumed with passion to notice my presence. I almost slipped as I fled the scene of the crime, feeling guilty for simply having witnessed it. The complex was quite large so I began a fruitless search for Anita. I knew I had to find her and tell her what I'd seen. As I weaved my way onto the dancefloor I saw Tatiana with Erik. Her arms were locked around his neck and they were engaged in a sexy samba, moving rhythmically beneath the multicoloured disco lights. Transfixed on each other, they were shut off from the rest of the room in their own little bubble of sugary affection. *So much for keeping it a secret.* I felt a pang of jealousy. Of course, I was happy for my friend but at that time envy often seeped into my heart when I saw anyone who had a rosy love life, or being honest, a love life full stop.

I decided the cure was a few shots of vodka. The sharp afterburn from the alcohol instantly numbed the pain. At the far side of the bar the Spaniard who'd accosted me in the pool was entwined in a passionate embrace with some petite blond girl. My eyes narrowed in disgust. He'd clearly found a more willing victim.

Eventually, after scouring the place I found Anita in the changing rooms, on the floor, slumped against a locker and hugging her knees to her chest. Her head was drooped but I could tell she was quietly weeping. *Shit, she knows.* Selfishly, I was relieved that the onus to tell her wasn't on me. No one likes to be the bearer of bad news.

'Hey' I said as I approached her tentatively.

She looked up. Despite the flushed cheeks and red eyes her face was still a marvel. If anything, crying seemed to have added a softness to her features, a fierce and raw kind of beauty.

'It's Edward, he's he's...'

Before she could finish she burst into loud fractured sobs, knocking her head backwards against the lockers.

'It's ok, I know' I confessed, crouching down next to her and putting my arm around her shoulders.

'What, how?' she asked, resting her head against my chest.

'I just saw them' I whispered.

'Yeah, me too' she said with a sniffle.

We sat in silence like that for a while, huddled on the cold floor, a dripping tap the only measure of time.

As we stood outside in the queue waiting to get on the coach back to Bologna, Edward swaggered over to us, brazenly flaunting his smug 'I just had sex' expression. Well, maybe that was just his normal expression, but it riled me nevertheless. I tensed up as he approached us, feeling the sudden urge to stand in front of Anita and protect her from his slimy charms.

'Hello girls, I was wondering where you'd gotten to. I've been looking all over' he said nonchalantly.

His shirt was unbuttoned to his waist and a towel was slung casually over his shoulder. Anita had her head bowed, unwilling to look him in the eye. Suddenly, a white hot rage took hold of me. Maybe it was because I was tired. Maybe it was because of my earlier encounter in the pool. Maybe it was because I'd had enough of the sickening sense of entitlement that made guys think they could do whatever the hell they liked, but the next thing I knew my fist was impacting Edward's face, crunching against his nose. I was shocked by my own strength. I'd never punched anyone in the face before. It was exhilarating. I recoiled by hand and looked at my blood splattered knuckles with a sense of wonder, as though they belonged to someone else. Edward clutched his nose in horror as Anita stared at me, wide-eyed and awestruck. I realised the rest of the party-goers were also looking our way, shocked into silence.

'*È uno stronzo traditore!*' I announced loudly, like a proud gladiator who'd just slain a lion.

A ripple of applause broke out and shouts of '*Brava!*' rang in my ears.

'I think she's broken my fucking nose!' squealed Edward, in a vain attempt to solicit some sympathy from the crowd.

Everyone laughed drunkenly, showing little concern. No one likes a cheating scumbag. Anita slept during the coach ride home, her head gently resting on my shoulder whilst Edward, sour-faced and moody, nursed his injury on the back seat. The red head had made him a makeshift bandage from a pair of knickers which looked utterly ridiculous. She cooed and fussed over him, but he ungratefully batted her away, like she was a mosquito.

I looked at Anita, angel-faced and serene in her repose and wondered how any man could treat such a marvel of creation as disposable. Like nothing more than a cheap razor or a fag end.

I stroked her hair with tenderness, hoping her dreams were more just than reality. She mumbled something incoherent as she adjusted her position. I noticed she was dribbling a little but I didn't mind.

'It's ok my love, Kerry's here and I'll never let you down' I soothed.

'Rest now, just rest.'

Chapter 10

It's funny how much breaking someone's nose can bring people together. When I told Ronan about it he gave me a high five and said, 'Wow K-dog who knew you were such a wee hard woman!'

Edward's betrayal hadn't exactly come as a shock. For Ronan the only downside to joining Anita and I's alliance against him was that he'd have to find someone else to pawn cigarettes off on nights out.

Together we rallied around Anita in her time of need, medicating her post-break up grief with shots of tequila and hours of drunken bullshitting in Piazza Verdi. We often scheduled study sessions in the university's glorious oak panelled library and met up before lectures for a quick chat and espresso. On weekends, when we weren't nursing hangovers we'd sometimes go shopping and afterwards, dressed in Armani dresses or Dolce and Gabbanna suits that we'd later return, we'd engage in our own mock fashion shoots around Bologna, soliciting odd looks from passers-by. Ronan mostly enjoyed playing the role of artistic director, screaming 'beautiful dah-ling!', 'I need more oomph!' or 'Work it sister!' where appropriate. We became a dynamic trio now that Erik and Tatiana were sickeningly in love and Marc was becoming increasingly elusive. I hadn't seen him since our 'date' and was in quandry as to what I should do next. I felt it was his turn to make the next move. The ball was in his court.

It was about this time that everything sort of fell into place for me, academically anyway. I no longer found my classes discombobulating and could understand mostly everything. I even developed a bit of a rapport with my Italian linguistics lecturer Signor Lombardi, a tall dapper looking man with a thinning hairline and heavy horn-rimmed glasses. By that I mean, he remembered my name as opposed to just calling me *La Irlandesa* and sometimes even asked me how I was getting on. I've always had an inherent need to be liked. It's pitiful really but all I needed was the tiniest bit of praise and I clung to it like a life raft. It was usually on those days when I'd had a class with Signor Lombardi that I'd go straight to the Emerald afterwards to study. Buoyed up by his encouraging words, I'd find that I could blast through my work with ease whilst Ronan and I spoke through furtive glances, not wishing to arouse Mario's ire.

It was on one such night that I was sitting on a tall stool at the bar, sipping the last dregs of my beer and waiting for Ronan to finish. It was three o'clock in the morning. All the chairs had been stacked neatly on top of the mahogany tables and he was diligently sweeping the floor, clearing up the debris of crisp crumbs and dust. The only customers left were me and a loved-up couple who lingered in a corner booth, clearly unable to take a hint.

'Ronan, *la spazzatura*!' barked Mario, clapping his hands sharply to indicate that it was Ronan's turn to take out the rubbish.

Ronan rolled his eyes but did as he was told. As usual, he stood with a furrowed brow, wrestling with a new bin liner in a hopeless attempt to find the opening. It was torturous to watch but the last time I'd tried to help, Mario had glared at me with such hatred that I'd stumbled with fright and subsequently knocked a glass off the bar, shattering it into a thousand tiny pieces. Needless to say, he was *not* happy.

When Ronan was finally released for the night, we bounded out the door, slamming it so hard as we left that the frosted glass rattled in its frame.

'Sorry about that K-dog. I actually thought I'd get away early tonight.' said Ronan as we walked arm in arm down a cobbled alley towards Piazza San Francesco.

'Oh, it's alright, just means we've got more drinking to do to make up for lost time.'

'Aye you're right there' he said, shoving me playfully. Our vibrant laughter echoed off the russet buildings, sending sparks of youthful energy into the peaceful night.

Bologna in the early hours of the morning is a sight to behold. Shades of red fade to hazy yellows and burnt oranges as the glow of street lamps illuminates the piazzas and quiet side streets. I'd been in Bologna for three months but it's beauty never failed to dazzle me.

As we passed Piazza Maggiore I took a moment to gaze up at the starry sky and utter a silent prayer of gratitude to the universe. Everything from the facade of San Petronio to the bronze sculpture of a coquettish lady in the adjoining via IV novembre looked like an elaborate work of art. Sometimes, when I was in a particularly dreamy mood, I liked to imagine that if I poured a glass of water on the scene it would vanish, the colours melting away like paint on a canvas.

When we reached the packed-out bar in Piazza San Francesco, we wasted no time in jostling to the front and ordering the highest percentage IPA on offer. It was quite a trendy place, a lot more boisterous than the Emerald with a distinctly younger clientele. I didn't usually like loud places, but the bustling atmosphere offered a certain amount of privacy, allowing us to blend in anonymously and talk without being overheard.

After about six pints Ronan's cheerful demeanour slipped as he stared vacantly into his pint. My immediate reaction was to panic. He didn't usually pass into the depression stage of drunk and I had the feeling that how I handled this moment would be a pivotal test of my character and worthiness as a friend.

'Is everything alright?' I ventured.

'God Kerry, my relationship's a mess' he said, putting his head in his hands and gripping fistfuls of his scruffy blond hair. I was a bit surprised since the last time he'd mentioned Rosie it was to say that she was coming to Bologna for a visit. He'd seemed thrilled about it.

'What do you mean?' I asked softly, lightly touching his forearm.

'Well, for one thing we've never even had sex.'

I paused for a moment, slightly taken aback. I suppose I'd just assumed that nobody our age was still a virgin, that everyone was a sexual virtuoso.

'Oh, right well that doesn't mean it's a mess' I offered.

'Doesn't it?'

Ronan's furrowed brow relaxed slightly as his eyes shone with new hope.

'No, of course not!' I stated emphatically.

I actually admired couples who took it slow and didn't rush into the physical side of things. My own experience had taught me that getting drunk and having sex on the first date usually didn't work out.

'You're obviously doing something right, I mean how long have you been together?' I asked.

'Six months' he said doubtfully as though he couldn't decide whether that was long or short.

'See! I've never even had a relationship that's lasted longer than a month' I confessed, glancing down at my beer.

He smiled at me sympathetically and I laughed to show that it wasn't a big deal. I wasn't supposed to be making this about me.

'Have you spoken to her about it, I mean is there any particular reason why you haven't had sex yet?' I asked, determined to offer some helpful advice.

'It's because, well you see it's because…' his voice strained as he struggled to get the words out.

I gulped, sensing that he was about to reveal something that I wasn't sure I was ready to know. It was a point of no return, that scene in the film that you'd masochistically rewind over and over.

He bowed his head a little and then looked up at me stoney-faced.

'You see it's because when I was little something really bad happened to me. At school there was this priest and he…' he trailed off, unable to finish but I knew exactly what he meant.

'Hey Ronan it's ok, I get it, you don't need to say it' I said, putting my arm around his shoulders. I felt sick to my stomach. For a moment I was lost for words so instead tuned into the sounds of clinking glasses and cacophonous chatter.

'I tried to kill myself once' I said suddenly. The words just slipped out. I didn't know what else to say. I'd always felt that emotional pain was like bartering. If someone opened up the darkest recesses of their soul to you, there was an unwritten rule that you had to offer something in return.

'Really?' he asked, eyes wide with fear and concern.

'Yeah, it was a couple of years when I'd just started uni.'

'Oh, Jesus, how?' he whispered.

He shifted on his barstool so he could look me in the eye but I avoided his gaze and returned to staring into my beer.

'Well, I took about fifty tablets, mostly epilepsy meds I stole from my roommate and a handful of painkillers.'

'Shit, Kerry', he said, his face a blend of shock and intrigue.

Saying it out loud was always strangely chilling. Even after extensive counselling I struggled to accept that it had really happened to *me*. I always felt like I was talking about someone else, a character in a book or someone I'd seen on tv. We sat in comfortable silence for a few minutes as rowdy Italians shunted us against the bar, eager to get served. My phone buzzed. It was a text from Anita.

'Hey, do you fancy meeting up with Anita? She's up for coming out' I asked, hoping the night wasn't lost, that we could still lift the mood.

'Yeah sure' he said, rolling up the sleeves of his black shirt as though preparing for battle.

'Great, I'll let her know' I said.

Then we exchanged a look, smiling timidly as though we'd seen each other naked or something. I suppose in a way we had.

We met Anita in front of the square's Basilica and she skipped towards us with open arms, eagerly engaging us in a group hug.

'Oh God, you don't know how happy I am to see you guys' she gushed, pulling us closer.

'Are love's young dream at it again?' asked Ronan with a cheeky wink.

'Yes, it's awful' she said exhaling melodramatically.

'There's only so long I can hide out in the kitchen for, only so many coffees I can make! I get that they're still in their honeymoon phase, but we only have two rooms in our apartment and the walls are really thin!'

She laughed giddily but her smile masked a deeper hurt and I felt a pang of annoyance towards Tatiana for her lack of tact.

'Right, we need to get you drunk woman, come on!' I ordered.

Ronan nodded his agreement as all three of us gleefully linked arms, with me in the middle, as we strode purposefully into the night. The scent of Anita's perfume filled my head with subtle notes of vanilla and jasmine as the crescent moon smiled down on us like a silver dagger.

We didn't really know where we were going but after a few twists and turns we stumbled across a bar called *Lo Scorpione*. At first it didn't appear to be open; the metal shutter was pulled halfway down. But on closer inspection we could hear voices and the soft hum of music radiating from within. One by one we ducked under the shutter to find ourselves in what I would later refer to as Bologna's best hidden treasure.

It was an Aladdin's cave with tea lights in glass jars on every table and posters covering every inch of the walls. Most of them were Scorpion related and I appreciated the subtle humour in that they had a portrait of Sting. There was also a real scorpion in a tank in the corner but it didn't seem to move so I assumed it was dead. A podgy man with a long greasy black ponytail wearily manned the bar and only gave a cursory glance in our direction as we came in.

We chose a table in the corner and after ordering some drinks were thrilled to find a shelf stacked with board games. After a few rounds of Jenga we switched to chess because I was getting too drunk and kept knocking the whole thing over prematurely. The only other customers were a curly haired man and well-dressed blond woman who slowly sipped their red wine, eyeing us curiously from across the bar.

'Checkmate!' shouted Ronan victoriously as he beat me for the third time in a row.

'Well done' said Anita. A gentle smile played about her lips as she lifted her tired eyes up from a dusty book she'd found entitled Scorpio: Master of the Zodiac.

'It's not fair' I said, slumping back in my rickety chair, feigning a sulk.

'How come you're so good at this?'

Ronan fiddled with his white knight and grinned sardonically.

'Well, there was a priest at my school who ran a chess club. He taught me everything I know.'

He paused to down the last of his rum as the darkness returned to his demeanour.

'But then he got arrested for child abuse so...'

'He knew where to put his pieces' I blurted.

The words escaped me before I had the chance to think. I involuntarily held my breath, waiting for Ronan's response but to my relief he snorted a laugh and playfully slapped the table. Anita raised an eyebrow in confusion.

'Ah K-dog what are ye like' he said and smiled warmly at me before leaving the table to go in search of the loo.

He was back to looking like the Ronan I knew and loved, my dear friend who harboured a tragic secret. It pained me to think of someone intentionally causing harm to such a beautiful soul.

I turned my attention to Anita who had now set her book to one side and was swilling her whiskey around in its glass.

'So, tell me, how are you doing?' I said woozily, reaching out to take her hand in mine.

'I'm fine' she said flatly, shrugging her shoulders.

'Come on hon, really? It can't be easy with Tatiana and Erik being all lovey dovey all the time after what happened.'

She sighed as the mask slipped and her eyes welled with pain.

'Well it's not easy. None of this is easy. My heart's breaking and I'm so angry and so mad. One moment I feel like I want to kill Edward and the next I break down in tears, wondering why I wasn't enough. Why wasn't I enough Kerry? Am I not pretty enough? Not skinny enough? What does that Bitch have that I don't?'

I shuffled my chair closer so I could put my arm around her as she gently cried into my shoulder.

'There there, shhhh. It's alright. It's alright.' I said, wishing I was a bit more sober.

'Listen, there's nothing wrong with you hon. You're beautiful and smart and funny. If Edward couldn't see that then that's his loss, right? Fuck him, Fuck everyone that doesn't see you for the dazzling, amazing human being that you are.'

She laughed between sobs as I stroked her silky soft hair.

'Do you really mean that?' she said gazing up at me.

Her eyes glistened like crystal pools.

'Of course. You're perfect' I said before kissing her on the forehead.

At this point Ronan returned from the toilets with slightly red eyes and I wondered if he'd been crying too.

'Aw Anita love what's wrong?' he asked tenderly as he sat down next to us again.

'It's nothing' she said, smiling whilst wiping tears from her eyes.

He shot me a worried glance, but I nodded as thought to say, 'I've got this.'

'So anyway', said Anita, eager to change the subject.

'What's happening with you and Marc?'

'Oh aye, how's that going?' said Ronan, rubbing his hands together with glee.

They listened intently as I recalled the semi-successful date that wasn't really a date and asked them for their advice.

Their consensus was that I should 'play the game' and be 'subtly obvious' about my intentions which seemed like a contradiction. I'd never been very good at flirting and didn't want to make a fool out of myself but Ronan agreed to go on a reconnaissance mission to uncover Marc's true feelings.

It was now five in the morning and we were the only customers in the place. It was still possible to order pizza and the barman obliged when we asked, albeit somewhat begrudgingly.

By the time we stepped back onto the street I felt like we'd been sucked into an alternate reality, some magical dimension and were now returning to the real world and current timeline. But the alcohol probably had something to do with that.

We parted ways in Piazza Maggiore which was now still and peacefully silent. As Anita broke off to go home I hugged Ronan once more and said, 'Hey, mate if you ever want to talk about anything, just let me know ok?'

He smiled, nodding his assent and I wondered if he regretted opening up to me.

'You too K-dog, you too' he said, supressing a yawn.

I didn't have my bike with me so I strolled home slowly through the empty streets, content for once to be alone with my thoughts and the sound of my footsteps. As cats yowled in the dark and the stars glinted overhead, I pondered life and how beautiful it was, with all its messiness and complications.

When I got home Barbara was snoring loudly in the living room and the fridge was making its usual whirring noise. I tucked myself into bed and drifted off to sleep in my tranquil blue room, hoping to dream of adventure and romance but, as was often the case, I ended up having a fitful sleep and a jagged nightmare that I wouldn't remember upon awakening.

Chapter 11

By mid-December, there was a chill in the air as Bologna turned festive. A tall Christmas tree strung with red and white lights stood proudly on the edge of Piazza Maggiore and stalls selling panettone, polenta, marzipan, handmade soap and a range of other delights stretched along the length of Via dell'Independenza. I liked the calm joviality of it all. It felt like the true spirit of Christmas, not the usual capitalist commercialised fanfare that I was used to at home.

Around this time, I managed to get myself a gig in a bar on Via dell Pratello. When I reached out on Facebook I didn't expect to hear back but was pleasantly surprised when they offered me a slot at their open mic night.

Arriving early to La Bandiera, I found the place empty and an elderly man with frizzy grey hair whom I presumed to be the owner was slumped over a table, glass of whiskey in hand.

'Ciao, Buona sera', I shouted.

He roused from his slumber and I explained why I was there.

After staring blankly for a moment he nodded and guided me to a room upstairs where I could store my guitar until it was time to start. A bare lightbulb hung from the ceiling and a dirty mattress was wedged in the corner between stacks of books, newspapers and a dusty piano. I wondered if this was where he slept.

We exchanged pleasantries and I was a little concerned that Federico had no recollection of our online exchange.

'Ah Giulia, *la ragazza* who works here, she takes care of all that' he said as he waved his hand lazily and grinned revealing a gold tooth.

The gang were coming to see me perform so I hoped I wouldn't disappoint. It had been months since I'd played in front of a proper audience – not counting my impromptu jam at the Amici. I'd been busking around the city quite a bit though, making a reasonable amount of cash, especially on Saturday nights. Italians seemed to love the novelty of a musician who sang in English and it warmed my heart to put a smile on the faces of passers-by.

It was still an hour until the show was due to start and I'd agreed to meet the others at the Emerald beforehand. But Federico had other ideas. When I said I was Irish his face lit up and he gripped my shoulder with a grubby hand.

'*Ah Irlanda, che verde!, che bella paese!*' he enthused, slurring his words slightly. I tried to make my excuses to leave but he bid me to stay and put on a video tape as an old set-top TV buzzed to life. It was a recording of U2 playing at Live Aid in 1985.

He smiled and looked to me for my reaction. I smiled back politely, impatiently twisting my hands. The others were waiting for me. Eventually I managed to escape after begrudgingly singing a few lines of With or Without You with him.

By the time I returned with the others the place was heaving with people. I gulped. The heat of bodies and the subtle scent of sweat mingled with liquor was nauseating. A knot formed in my stomach and Anita, sensing my fear smiled at me and squeezed my hand.

'Don't worry, I'm sure you'll be great' she said, giving me a soft peck on the cheek. Her breath smelt like cinnamon.

Ronan's girlfriend Rosie was over visiting for the week; a pale, thin girl with raven curls and scarlet lips. She was striking. From the few words we'd exchanged at The Emerald I'd deduced that she was studying English at Trinity College in Dublin and had met Ronan on a student union night out. I already knew these things since Ronan had told me a little about her but I was trying to be polite and make conversation. I've never been very *au fait* with small talk.

When I'd told her that I was going to be singing some of my own songs which were inspired by my break-ups she said, 'Gentle lady do not sing sad songs about the end of love, lay aside sadness and sing how love that passes is enough.'

I stared at her blankly and she returned my gaze with a smug smile before explaining curtly, 'James Joyce.'

As she slowly sipped her vodka cranberry I could feel the jealousy emanating from her like a putrid stench. I laughed nervously and said I wasn't really a poetry fan while secretly thinking about all the words that rhyme with 'bitch.'

Ronan seemed all twitchy and uptight. He took her porcelain hand and pushed through the crowd to the bar. Anita followed them while Tatiana and Erik sat down at one of the tables arranged in front of the stage, unashamedly initiating a public display of affection. Marc was there too which added to my jitters. We hadn't really spoken properly since our 'date' and I wanted to impress him.

'Bonne Chance' he said with a wink when it was my time to perform, his hand lightly grazing my arm. I was dying to ask Ronan if he'd been successful in his sleuthing, but I'd have to wait until Rosie wasn't shooting daggers.

As I swung my guitar over my neck and took to the stage, butterflies tickled my stomach and the floorboards creaked under my black patent heels. I was wearing my dressiest dress; a blue velvet number which draped flatteringly over my curves. Sheer black tights and a shiny silver cat-shaped pendant completed the ensemble. I fiddled with it as I stepped up to the mic and introduced myself. Giulia, when I finally met her in person had explained that all the other acts had dropped out or not turned up so I would be performing a solo concert. No pressure then.

Looking out at the crowd I spotted my friends near the front. Anita gave me a reassuring thumbs up which settled me aa bit though my heart still beat wildly in my chest.

I sang a few covers to get warmed up, my usual favourites like Everything I do by Bryan Adams and a couple of Ed Sheeran songs. I was rewarded with applause and cheers after each number. I found my flow. Then I moved onto my own material which everyone enjoyed, except of course Rosie, who pursed her lips whilst territorially running her slender fingers through Ronan's hair. Anyone could have been mistaken for thinking I was singing love songs about her boyfriend. I tried to interchange between sad heartbreak numbers and my more upbeat tunes which spoke of cats, sex, love and whiskey.

Then as I was mid-song Federico interrupted me by shouting raggedly from across the bar 'I know your country better than you do!'

I paused. The whole room turned to look at him. He knocked a shot glass to the floor which shattered, breaking the silence.

'I worked for an Irish language newspaper during the troubles' he went on, now considerably more drunk than when I'd first met him.

My mouth gaped open. I didn't know how to respond. Then he fumbled to the other side of the bar, pulled something from a dusty shelf in the corner and swaggered up to the stage to present it to me. It was a framed picture of Bobby Sands, most likely a newspaper clipping. I froze in bemused panic.

My eyes drifted to Marc who was reclining in his chair with an air of amusement. He was wearing a midnight blue silk shirt and I briefly fantasised about ripping it open, straddling him and peeling off his tight black denim jeans.

I snapped out of it, remembering that everyone, including Frederico, was staring at me with bated breath. Then I spent about ten minutes trying to explain the 1981 Irish hunger strike in Italian to a room full of tipsy punters who had just come out to hear a bit of music. I won't bore you with the history and politics of it all, I'll leave you to research that for yourself if you're so inclined. All I will say is that it's the most absurd experience I've ever had at a gig. I eventually got back to singing and towards the end I even took some requests.

I begrudgingly finished with a rendition of Alanis Morissette's Ironic which infuriates me since the lyrics are semantically incorrect. What's ironic about rain on your wedding day? Sounds like just my luck.

Afterwards while I was in the bathroom washing my hands and still riding the wave of the post-gig high, I overhead Ronan and Rosie arguing. The adjoining narrow hallway was quite echoey and easily carried the spiteful jibes and flustered replies. I sighed. I didn't want to make life difficult for Ronan or cause tension in his relationship, even though I knew I'd done nothing wrong. He was the first close male friend I'd ever had and I hoped with all my heart that Rosie wouldn't deliver the ultimatum 'Me or her.'

A door slammed and I tentatively crept out of the bathroom. Ronan was slumped against the cream brick wall, his head tipped back in woe. When he saw me, he sprung back to life and hugged me tight, showering me with compliments about my performance. I didn't mention the tiff. It wasn't the time or place for me to play relationship counsellor, especially since I suspected that I was the cause of the conflict.

I quickly said my goodbyes, not wanting to be caught up in any drama. Anita accompanied me for part of the walk home which was slow since I'd forgotten to pack my flats and had to tentatively pick my way through the cobbles. As we passed under the glittering Christmas lights of Piazza Maggiore she said, 'I saw Edward the other day.'

'Oh really?' I replied, half-feigning surprise.

'Yeah he was with *her* in the library. Kissing. No shame.'

'Oh hon I'm so sorry' I said. My heart stung on her behalf.

'It's ok, I know I'm too good for him anyway.' An impish smile spread across her face in the pale moonlight.

'Too right' I concurred.

I took her hand and although encumbered by heels and a guitar, skipped with her around Neptune's fountain which spluttered gleefully. The bell of San Petronio cathedral chimed midnight as our laughter dispersed into the crisp night air.

When I got home I hastily kicked off my shoes and was assailed by a flurry of excited questions from Barabara, asking me how it had gone. Once I'd escaped to the solace of my room I noticed I had a text from Marc which read 'Well done tonight, you were great! Xx.'

Two kisses! I flopped into bed spent, a dreamy grin on my face. *Il m'aime aussi, peut-être?* Perhaps my love didn't have to be unrequited after all.

Chapter 12

'Pass the panettone *per favore*' said Tatiana, dabbing the corners of her mouth with a napkin.

The three of us, Tatiana, Anita and I were sat around Barbara's dining table where we'd just enjoyed a sumptuous Christmas dinner of cold cuts and cheeses followed by a main course of spinach and ricotta tortellini. I had a satisfying ache in my stomach and wasn't sure I could manage dessert.

Most Erasmus students went home for Christmas but I'd decided to stay in Bologna to save money on flights and the girls had done likewise. When I'd explained this to Barabara she'd jumped at the chance to cook dinner for us and wouldn't take no for an answer.

'Barbara, leave the washing up, we can do it later, I'll help you' I shouted into the kitchen, but she happily dismissed my concerns saying she wanted to keep busy.

The flat was gaily decorated with paper garlands of snowflakes and angels as well as twinkling multicoloured fairy lights. Anita eyed the ceramic busts of Mussolini on the wall (which were now draped in tinsel) with a grin and poured herself a glass of Baileys. This was my contribution to the feast; an Irish home comfort I'd received in a package from mum. It perfectly complimented the rich sweet Italian bread.

After letting our food settle we made our way to The Emerald where Mario seemed a lot more jovial than normal. He even treated us to some free champagne. I said it was because he was in the Christmas Spirit but it was more likely due to the lack of customers.

Before I got too drunk I slipped away to answer a phone call from my mum. She was disappointed that I hadn't come home and made sure I knew about it. Her ultimate weapon in the guilt trip arsenal was to say that Toodles and Ginger, the cats, wished I was there. Then she had to go because they were attacking the Christmas tree. I rang my dad later but we didn't talk for very long since he was out hill walking somewhere in the remote countryside and bracing wind and didn't have very good phone reception.

When I returned we took it in turns to exchange gifts. For Tatiana I'd picked out a selection of sweets, truffles and Turkish delight and I got Anita a wooden yo-yo from the crafts market. She once mentioned her love for them and I thought this one, with the nativity scene painted on it, would be a welcome addition to her collection. Her face lit up with wonder when she unwrapped it and she expressed her gratitude by ordering me another drink. Tatiana had hand knitted me a beautiful violet scarf and from Anita I received a set of souvenir shot glasses.

'These should come in handy' I said happily, as I kissed and hugged them both, thanking them for their gifts.

In the evening we huddled around my laptop in bed, eating sweets and watching old Laurel and Hardy videos. Surprisingly, it was Tatiana's idea who revealed she had a love of old British slapstick humour. I pulled my cosy duvet tight around us as we laughed and chatted late into the night.

***

New Year's Eve crept up unexpectedly. Most of the Erasmus students had returned by then and I found myself at a masquerade party in Marc's flat. It was actually Marc and Ronan's flat now since one of the students had vacated, freeing up a room. Having put up with the Amici's dodgy plumbing for so long, Ronan jumped at the chance to move in. Everyone there was wearing a mask. Some were lacy and sensual, others comical, colourful and bizarre. Ronan had gone for a pirate eye-patch which I'm not sure technically fulfilled the dress code.

When I arrived I spotted him slumped on the lumpy brown sofa, wedged between a couple who were grinding on each other and a girl in a panda mask who'd already passed out. He looked dishevelled and was staring despondently into his beer. I invited him outside for some fresh air and he gladly accepted. As I exhaled wispy breath into the cold winter night he lit a cigarette and turned up the collar on his brown leather jacket.

'Rosie broke up with me' he said matter-of-factly in between puffs.

'Oh, I'm so sorry Ronan' I said as I tentatively patted him on the back, not quite knowing the appropriate response to the situation. A slight pang of guilt gnawed at my stomach. *Was I to blame in some way?* I took off my purple sequined mask and twisted it about in my hands.

'I told her and she couldn't handle it' he said after a few moments, a slight strain in his voice.

I didn't need to ask him what 'it' was. I hugged him tightly since no words I had could have sufficed.

Once we got back inside he perked up a little and urged me to finally tell Marc how I felt. His reconnaissance mission had proved unsuccessful since all he'd deduced was that Marc thought I was 'nice' and 'a good singer.' *Tell me something I don't know.*

'You need to get a move on, it's now or never Kerry' he said, poking me playfully in the ribs.

For once I agreed with him. It was now 10pm and with any luck I'd be French kissing by midnight. And I didn't mean air kisses.

Every inch of the small living space was packed with people and I couldn't pick Marc out of the crowd. Then I heard a commotion in the kitchen and went in to find Erik down on one knee in front of Tatiana, proffering a diamond ring. She was wearing a black lace mask which made it seem as though a butterfly had landed on her face. I gasped in shock and squeezed into a gap between the fridge and the oven, standing on my tiptoes to get a better view.

'Will you marry me?' asked Erik. The assembled crowd drew an audible breath.

Tatiana squealed her response as the room burst into joyous applause. They embraced and shared a sensual kiss before accepting congratulations from both friends and strangers. Erik looked gangly and awkward as he shook proffered hands, but also blissfully happy. They both did. I spotted Anita sitting on top of the worktop sipping a glass of white wine, a smile painfully painted on her face. Her white feather mask made her look like she'd just stepped off the stage of an opera. From her lack of surprise I deduced that she must have known about the plan beforehand.

I thought they were crazy but I hugged them all the same whilst muttering stunned felicitations. Tatiana, her face aglow with excitement, promised I'd be invited to the wedding. *Yeah, if you haven't broken up by then*, I thought. It makes me sad to think I was so young yet so cynical. In fact, they proved a lot of people wrong and are still happily married now, three decades later. I was just jealous.

I eventually found Marc and slyly invited him out onto the roof for a 'chat', using the excuse that the music was too loud to hear him. After some general small talk where we discussed how we'd spent Christmas, if we'd received any nice presents etc., I decided to go in for the kill.

'So, Marc there's something I've been meaning to tell you for a while' I ventured, wishing I'd had just a little bit more to drink.

'Mmm?' he replied curiously. A deep indigo mask framed his eyes and he looked very dapper in a stylish shirt and waistcoat. He set down his beer, eyeing me expectantly.

In the end I decided that actions speak louder than words, so I reached up behind his neck and pulled him into a clumsy kiss. My tongue only ventured inside his mouth briefly before he pushed me away, laughing.

'Kerry, I think you've had too much to drink' he said as he tried to compose himself enough to light a cigarette.

Hurt, I felt the tears begin to well up in my eyes. At least I was wearing a mask.

'I like you' I said feebly, 'I've just been waiting for the right moment to tell you.'

In genuine surprise he replied 'What? Since when?'

'Since Ravenna' I mumbled. The cold air numbed my extremities and I wished I'd put on my coat so I wouldn't have to be both freezing and humiliated.

'Ah *desolé*, I think you're great but...'

He had the mercy to spare me the end of that sentence as he stared down awkwardly at his suede brogues.

Silence hung thick in the air between us as the babble of boisterous revellers drifted up from the street below. I excused myself to go to the bathroom where I locked myself in and sat silently weeping on the toilet. *But what? But you're fat, but I don't find you attractive, but you're not my type.* After ten minutes there was a knock on the door.

'Just a minute' I shouted.

They knocked again, more urgently this time. I sighed in frustration and hurriedly dabbed my eyes with some toilet paper. I unlocked the door to find a very tipsy looking Anita.

'Shit Kerry you look awful, what happened?' she asked. She didn't look so great herself.

She joined me in the bathroom and we sat in either ends of the mint green tub, legs awkwardly akimbo. Anita had to hitch her tight black dress up to her waist so her red lacy underwear was on show. The taps dug uncomfortably into my back as I explained what happened. She consoled me with the loving offer of whiskey from her hip flask which I gratefully accepted, and she confessed that she was feeling a twinge of envy over Tatiana's engagement.

'It's just that it's always *her*, you know? She's always the one that gets the guy and I'm, well I'm left standing there...in her shadow' she said woozily before letting a hiccup escape.

We cried together and laughed together and eventually after a queue formed outside we decided it was time to re-join the party.

We danced to a playlist of The Beatles, U2, Vanessa Paradis and Fleetwood Mac. It seemed that Ronan and Marc had both had an equal hand in choosing the music. When I Don't Wanna miss a Thing by Aerosmith came on, Anita and I slow danced, drunkenly stepping on each other's toes. I wrapped my arms around her soft neck and she gripped my waist as we half-waltzed, periodically chuckling when we bumped into the white plastic Christmas tree.

Around 11pm I was shocked to spot Edward and his redhead among the other guests (who I discovered was a Latvian girl named Kristina). They were casually holding court in the living room, laughing and joking like they had every right to be there. I glared at him with pure malice and he ignored me, purposefully avoiding my gaze. When I found out that Marc had invited him a wave of anger welled up and unleashed my nasty drunk.

'What are you doing here? You need to leave', I hissed, storming up to him.

'Look we're not here to cause any trouble, alright. Just chill' he sniggered.

If it hadn't been for Ronan holding me back I probably would have swung for him and broken his nose again. Kristina at least had the decency to look ashamed. I wanted to get rid of him before Anita realised he was there but it was too late. She stumbled across the spectacle which now had quite the audience, a look of shock and pity on her face.

'Kerry leave it, he's not worth it' she said, touching me gently on the arm.

But just as we turned to walk away I heard Edward snort under his breath, 'frigid bitch.'

A switch flicked in Anita's head and she spun round, resourcefully grabbing the nearest drink to hand and unceremoniously flinging it in his face.

'Fucking hell!' he yelled, 'so you're not just a prude you're fucking crazy too!'

The Campari dripped down his front, forming a satisfying blood-red stain on his white shirt.

No one seemed to have the least bit of sympathy. Erik eventually ushered them out, diplomatically playing the part of bouncer.

At ten minutes to midnight I quickly surveyed the party. Everyone was mostly coupled up now, ready to welcome in the New Year. Marc and Ronan seemed to be having an intense chat on the sofa. I couldn't see Anita anywhere.

Stepping into the kitchen I spotted a tall guy, fairly well built, leaning against the fridge. He was wearing an emerald green mask with a black lace trim that nicely framed his hazel eyes.

'Alright everyone, get ready for the countdown!' shouted Marc from the other room. It was now or never.

With more confidence than I felt, I strode over to the mysterious stranger and locked my arms around his neck pulling him closer to me. He opened his mouth to say something but I silenced him, putting a finger to his lips.

'Shhh' I said. I wasn't there to talk.

As the countdown began, I stepped up on my tiptoes positioning my lips an inch away from his. At the count of 'one' it was him who made the move, kissing me tenderly yet with a passion that fired up my heart.

When we finally broke apart I reached up to peel back his mask. I gasped. He smiled mischievously. It was James! Those lips that had kissed me so expertly belonged to James! My American Knight in shining armour.

He walked me home through the icy streets as fireworks crackled far off in the distance, heard but not seen. Once we reached my front door I considered inviting him in. The cool air had sobered me a bit but I was still considerably drunk.

'Happy new year James' I said, smiling like a loon. 'And thanks for walking me home.'

'Happy new year Kerry' he replied, showing a line of perfect white teeth.

'And hey, no sweat, at least you didn't need an ambulance this time' he laughed.

I leant forward on the doorstep and gave him a final kiss goodnight under the soft glow of the outside light.

We exchanged numbers and I breathed a sigh of content as I watched him turn and step back into the crisp velvet night. He strode confidently, but not cockily. A *true* gentleman. *Perhaps this year was off to a good start after all.* I could only hope.

Chapter 13

My birthday is on the 16th January which sometimes also happens to be Blue Monday; the most depressing day of the year. It's also the time when my all friends are usually broke, the weather is dire, and no one wants to go out or do anything. When Anita found out my birthday was coming up she graciously invited me to a 'Russian dinner' at her place where we could all gather to jointly celebrate Tatiana and Erik's engagement and the fact I'd survived another year.

The girls' apartment was cramped yet homely with Ikea pot plants, hardwood floors, wicker furniture and a pink shag pile rug. It was open plan with the living and dining area occupying one space whilst the small kitchen was sectioned off behind a beaded curtain. It had the aura of a gypsy caravan. The sofa converted into a bed and the other sleeping area was accessed by a short flight of stairs where a mattress was enclosed by wooden planks. It wasn't quite an attic room, or a bunk bed, more like a comfortable shelf.

In addition to the girls and I, Marc, Ronan and Erik were also there. I made sure to sit at the other end of the table from Marc, still embarrassed about what had happened on New Year's Eve. We hadn't spoken since but we air-kissed and he wished me 'Happy Birthday' on arrival, so he didn't seem to be too phased by it. When Erik wasn't gazing dreamily into Tatiana's eyes I managed to get to know him a little better. The most interesting fact gleaned was that he wanted to go pro as a volleyball player and was hoping to make it onto the national team when he returned to Sweden.

'I study economics but that's just to appease my father. My heart's really in the game...and here of course' he said pointing to Tatiana's chest.

She put her arm around him and affectionately rubbed the thumb-print birthmark on his neck as she nuzzled his shoulder.

I looked over at Ronan and had to supress a laugh. He was gesturing pretending to be sick. Marc rolled his eyes and sighed as he tore off a piece of bread.

'Ta-da!, Here's the *Pelmeni!*' announced Anita, grinning proudly as she brought out a casserole dish from the kitchen.

It was an appetising delicacy of meat-filled pastry dumplings, served in a soup broth. We all dug in and afterwards enjoyed a course of straight vodka shots. I'd thought Anita had been kidding about this when she first explained the premise of a 'Russian dinner'.

After that, despite having lined our stomachs we all got a bit loose. Ronan started singing ABBA songs with Marc providing the harmonies as they hilariously swayed back and forth, arms interlocked. It was the most drunk I'd ever seen Marc since he was usually perfectly composed no matter how much he'd had to drink. Erik claimed to hate ABBA and started playfully throwing mandarin oranges at them which he picked out of the fruit bowl. Ronan returned fire whilst chiding that Ireland has won Eurovison more times than Sweden.

'Aye right, ABBA is pure shite compared to Johnny Logan!' he chided playfully.

Then Tatiana stood up to belly dance on one of the wicker chairs, accidentally stamping a hole through it.

At this point Anita invited me to see her 'bedroom' so I followed her up the little steps onto the shelf. She had a black and white poster of Audrey Hepburn taped to the ceiling above, that iconic shot of her smoking from Breakfast at Tiffany's. I lay down next to her, my face barely an inch from hers as we talked drunken nonsense. I asked her to teach me some Russian and she made me repeat the words for, 'hello', 'cockroach' and 'book.' In my mind my pronunciation was superb. She asked me if I knew any Irish and I had to confess that I only remembered a few phrases from a class I'd been forced to take in school. I relayed what I could remember, and she said it was like music. She tucked a piece of her hair back and for the first time I was close enough to notice a tiny tattoo of a sun behind her left ear. She smelt so good. Then an unexpected thought danced across my mind. *What would it be like to kiss Anita?*

I'd never really had an inclination towards girls save for a few drunken forays back at uni. But right then, in that moment, gazing softly into her pale grey eyes that glistened like moonstone, I felt a flicker of desire stir in the pit of my stomach. She really was beautiful. Not just pretty but jaw-dropping, cross your heart beautiful, like a model from a Pre-Raphaelite painting. Then a mandarin orange hit the side of my head with a light thud and the spell was broken.

'Oi, are you two coming down or what?' yelled Ronan. He was now juggling two oranges and contemplating adding a third into the mix. I admired his dexterity after so much vodka.

'Hold your ponies we're coming now' said Anita before elegantly climbing down the steps and hastily smoothing her tight denim skirt. I smiled to myself. I always found her incorrect use of English idiom delightfully endearing.

Then we hit the town. We started off in Piazza Verdi where we smoked a bit of weed before trawling our favourite bars. Erik underwent a drastic transformation and for some reason started hating on my purse and calling it 'ugly.' It was fake Prada and quite stylish I'd thought. Marc and Ronan spent most of the night talking in hushed tones and slapping each other on the back affectionately. At one place we ended up chatting to this weird old guy who poked my stomach and asked, *'Aspetti uno bambino?'*

My face fell. The first time I'd been mistaken for being pregnant I'd been able to laugh it off but this time I was drunk and on an emotional knife edge. *Was I really that fat?* I ran inside to the bathroom and shut the door where I cried my eyes out for a solid ten minutes. It was becoming a pattern for me. Eventually Anita coaxed me out and consoled me by singing a Russian folk song as she hugged me in the rain. I soon forgot about the creepy man. Later I took my first ever drag of a cigarette. I'd assumed it was weed since they were all passing it around. It was actually just their last fag. The last thing I remember was finding a mattress lying incongruously in the street, which we all flopped onto, our limbs awkwardly overlapping. Fade to black.

***

My phone alarm buzzed me awake. As I rubbed my bleary eyes I reached out my hand to turn it off and to my horror, accidentally caressed Erik's naked bum. Startled, I looked to my right to see him and Tatiana lying next to me, completely naked and still in a deep sleep. A thin bedsheet had slipped down so it barely covered anything. I picked it up and tentatively laid it over them, preserving the modesty of Tatiana's erect nipples. I wondered if this counted as a threesome?

We were back in the girls' apartment on the sofa bed. My throat was parched and my head felt like it had been steamrolled. I woozily stood up and retrieved my phone from the dining table. After turning off the alarm I noticed I'd sent ten drunk texts – all of them to James. *Oh God*, I thought. I read through them, bracing myself for the worst. Thankfully most of them were unintelligible gibberish. But there was one, just one which clearly read 'I think I love you.'

Noooooo. This is awful. This is terrible. James will never want to see me again. Why would he? He'll think I'm a psycho. Maybe I am? Of course I don't love him, or do I? No! I barely know him! Why am I such an idiot? I felt sick. I knew I wouldn't make it to the bathroom in time so hastily grabbed my handbag, and emptied it on the table. The only things it contained were my ugly purse, keys, eye liner and a lipstick in a shade called wine not?

I refilled it with the contents of my stomach; mostly vodka scented bile and a trace of Pelmeni. I wiped my mouth with the back of my hand and tried to think clearly as I berated myself for my poor life choices.

While stumbling into the kitchen en route to the bathroom, I nearly tripped over Ronan. Now it was my turn to peel *him* off a tiled floor. We waited until Anita woke up (she'd actually made it into her own bed) before all heading out for some breakfast to ease our hangovers.

'Crazy night last night huh?' I said as I considered whether or not I could stomach a croissant.

Anita nodded her agreement as she picked absent-mindedly at her brioche. Her fingernails were painted jet black and her make up was perfectly preserved from the night before.

Ronan exhaled morosely as he stirred his tea. All of his joviality from the night before seemed to have evaporated.

'I miss her' he said, avoiding eye contact. I stretched a comforting hand across the table but he pulled away and shrugged his shoulders. Anita tried to give him a hug but he bolted to his feet and excused himself, mumbling something about meeting up with Marc. As I watched him leave, the bell on the door of the little trattoria jingled brightly. He hadn't even touched his Danish.

'I thought he was doing ok but it turns out I was wrong. I just wish there was something I could do, you know?' I said, frowning into my espresso.

'Yeah, I've barely seen him since he moved in with Marc' said Anita.

Her mood also seemed to have swung to the darker side of the spectrum. She didn't have to say anything. I sensed her fears of loneliness and being left behind once Tatiana and Erik went off to live their happily ever after.

When I told her about my drunk texts to James she laughed and her face lightened a little. She advised that the best course of action was to do nothing. I would probably end up doing more harm than good if I sent an apology text.

As I was washing my hands in the bathroom I saw a poster advertising free art classes. My interest was piqued. I'd always liked drawing and painting but it had been ages since I'd done anything like that. My mother had always discouraged my artistic side, saying that I should do something more 'productive.' When I returned I told Anita about the class and convinced her to try it out with me in the hope that it would lift her spirits.

***

A few days later after a long day of classes, Anita and I met in Piazza Maggiore to walk to the art class together. It was in an inconspicuous looking building with tall heavy wooden doors on the corner of Via Centotrecento. When we stepped inside it was very dark, lit only by candles placed here and there on shelves and in alcoves. The walls were covered in murals, most of which seemed to be of a political nature. A few people eyed us suspiciously.

We followed signs to the class and climbed up four flights of dimly lit stairs before we found it. The room was lined with several rows of desks and chairs and at the front a swarthy skinned, scruffy looking guy was drawing something on the chalk board.

'Ah benvenuti raggazze!' he said cheerfully as we arrived and took our seats.

He introduced himself as Omar and explained that we were going to be drawing the human body as he visually explained proportions on the board. Then Anita supressed a giggle as a tanned adonis stepped out from behind a screen and dropped his robe so we could have a full view of his perfectly sculpted body. My jaw dropped. It was Roberto! I couldn't believe it and pinched myself to make sure I wasn't dreaming. Blushing, I temporarily averted my gaze. When he spotted me he gave me a friendly wink and then positioned himself in a wide legged stance with one hand on his hip. I was equally embarrassed and aroused.

I hadn't anticipated a life drawing class. The other attendees didn't flinch and began sketching fervently with their pencils and charcoal. I didn't have a clue where to start but made a valiant effort of trying to capture both his rippling muscles and generously sized manhood. Anita's finished work was incredible, it was so realistic.

'Wow that's amazing', I said, tracing the outline of Roberto's form with my finger.

'Oh thanks, I used to take classes back in Russia', she replied modestly.

Omar also generously praised Anita's work. When he looked at mine he patted me on the back and said I'd made a 'good effort.'

I hung around afterwards to chat to him. He explained that the building used to belong to the hospital in Bologna but that it was now occupied by squatters and had been repurposed by the Young Communists' Society as an art and social space. He had a friendly yet slightly intense demeanour as he regarded me with deep set coffee-coloured eyes.

Roberto, now fully clothed asked me how I was doing and having seen him naked I was reduced to a squirming, stuttering wreck. Anita bit her lip to supress another onslaught of the giggles. That night as I returned home I told Barbara what I'd been doing.

'Ah *che fico*!, where?' she asked as she feverishly scrubbed the kitchen worktops.

It suddenly occurred to me that she wouldn't be pleased to know I'd been at a communist hangout but under pressure, in the moment, I couldn't think of any other venue. When I told her she froze, her whole body tensed.

'If it were me, I'd put a bomb under the whole thing' she said darkly before recommencing her cleaning, somewhat more violently than before. Lost for words, I quietly slipped away to my room.

Chapter 14

As I walked into the dining room one morning I noticed Barbara wasn't her usual chirpy self. Slumped in a chair she was nursing an espresso and staring vacantly ahead. She didn't even notice I was there at first. It was only when I said '*Buona mattina!*' that she snapped out of her trance and managed to mutter a 'Good morning' in return.

It was now February and the worst of the cold was over but remnants of frost still cast an icy glaze over the windows. As I sat down to eat my cereal I gently asked her what was wrong. She seemed reluctant to tell me, as though saying it out loud would make the sad truth all the more real. A heavy silence hung in the air between us before eventually she confided that she had a sick friend, a work colleague who was in hospital. She'd had a long battle with breast cancer and Barbara didn't know if she was going to make it.

I stretched across the table and gingerly took her hand in mine, squeezing it gently. I never knew how to react in moments like these but a physical gesture felt more meaningful than any useless words I could say. A single tear rolled down her cheek as she smiled at me weakly.

'Marina is my best friend. We've worked together for twenty years and now I might have to say goodbye to her forever. But it…it's too hard. I can't' she said, squeezing my hand back.

I offered her a tissue from the bathroom and she took it gratefully, sniffling into it and wiping her eyes.

'I'm so sorry Barbara' was all I could say.

I couldn't say what I was sorry for. It wasn't as though the situation was my fault. But I was sorry that this had to happen. Sorry that she had to lose someone so dear to her to such a cruel disease. Sorry that I couldn't say something more poignant and helpful. Sorry that 'Sorry' wasn't enough and never would be.

***

Anita never came back with me to the squatter's building but I continued attending the classes, trying to master the life of art drawing from my patient teacher Omar. But eventually I gave up. I was more of an abstract artist anyway. There was some blank space in the corridor leading to the art room. When I explained to Omar where my artistic strengths lay, he offered me the wall as my blank canvas to do with as I wished. I was thrilled.

'But doesn't it have to be, you know…communist related?' I asked.

'No, not at all. As long as it's pretty it's fine!' he assured.

So that was it. I set to work on an elaborate mural of cats, flowers and abstract patterns, executed in brightly coloured markers and paints. I was able to pop in to work on it whenever I liked. I didn't often see many other people since the families who squatted there all had their own rooms downstairs. Occasionally, a curious child would wander up to the top floor but was usually swiftly recalled and scolded by an anxious parent.

Once a month the group hosted an aperitivo in the building, a 'drink and draw' event where they'd serve drinks, play music and the artists could continue to work whilst being watched by a very chilled out audience. The money raised went towards paying for the electricity and other running costs of the building.

On one such evening I arrived to find a guitarist had already set up in one of the rooms and was happily strumming away. A small crowd had gathered around him, enraptured by his acoustic flair. Other artists were tending to their respective works, adding fine details and elaborate strokes on the rough walls. I bought myself a beer and set to work on my mural. I was aware that it was already drawing attention from some other members of the group since it was the only non-politically motivated piece, but I tried not to pay any heed to the whispers I heard behind my back.

I was adding some purples and blues into the chaotic patterns when a voice jolted me out of my artistic flow,

'Hey, need a bit of inspiration?'

I looked to me left and there was a frizzy haired Italian, crouched down next to me, grinning wildly and kindly offering me a spliff.

He introduced himself as Francesco and we got talking.

'So, cats and flowers, how did you come up with that concept?' he asked, intrigued.

I could have invented some elaborate metaphor for what the cats and flowers represented but instead I told him the truth, that they were simply two things I really liked. Then we moved onto other topics such as where I was from and what I was doing in Bologna. I briefly mentioned Barbara and her political leaning. He laughed and then paused as a sudden realisation dawned.

'Wait you're the Irish girl who lives with the fascist!' he exclaimed.

Slightly confused, I ventured that yes, I was she.

'*Porco Dio!*' he blasphemed. His mahogany eyes dilated as he flung his hands in the air, almost dropping his joint.

'You're that girl that we rang an ambulance for!'

I paused for a moment, slightly stunned as realisation dawned.

'And you're one of James' roomates!' I shot back. Then my sense of awe shifted into sudden panic as I wondered if he'd been told all about the psycho girl who thought she was in love with him after one kiss.

'Hey, here's here now if you want to say hello' said Francesco with a casual wink.

'*Ah, siiii? Che bene, perfetto*, I'd really like that' I replied nervously.

My paranoia told me he was mocking me.

Before I had time to come up with an exit strategy, Francesco had already beckoned James over. I hastily stood up, trying to compose myself as I wiped my paint splattered hands on my dungarees. James seemed very relaxed and sauntered towards us with one hand in his trouser pocket and the other holding a bottle of Peroni. He smiled brightly and greeted me a hug and kiss on the cheek. Francesco, clearly understanding the dynamic, decided to give us some privacy and slipped away to mingle.

'Well, hello, fancy seeing you here' I said, my voice rising two octaves above its normal pitch.

'Yeah, it's such a nice surprise! It's kind of funny. I've never been here before, but Francesco told me about the event, so I decided to tag along' he said, before taking a sip of his beer.

I eyed him curiously, trying to ascertain if he thought I was crazy or not. He certainly didn't seem uneasy. A new musician had just taken centre stage in the other room and was blasting out a heavy bass riff.

'I was actually thinking of calling you, the universe must have read my mind!' he said, smiling as he rubbed the back of his neck.

'Oh um, wow, ok, that's cool' I replied, tripping over my words.

'Yeah, I mean, it's cool if you don't want to but I was going to ask if you'd be up for going to get a drink with me sometime?' he asked, running his fingers over the lapel of his navy blazer jacket.

There was a significant pause as I struggled to consolidate my emotions of glee and shock. This was such a wild coincidence. It had to be fate! The butterflies swirled in my stomach as my excitement got the better of me.

'Yes! Yes, I'd absolutely love that! How about now?' I blurted.

He looked slightly taken aback but was still smiling as he suggested a nearby bar.

'Great! Just let me clean up a little in the loo and then we can go' I said, giving a thumbs up.

In the bathroom I scrubbed the paint off my hands and a few flecks from my brow and nose. I also patted my hair down with some water as it had gotten very frizzy in the humid gathering and hastily reapplied my lipstick and eye-liner. Luckily, I'd brought a change of clothes so was able to swap my dungarees for a nice red knitted jumper dress and tights. I smiled at myself in the grimy mirror with a resolve to be both cool and sexy. *Don't fuck this up Kerry, don't fuck this up.*

I was glad I'd been able to change since the place James picked was distinctly more high class than the establishments I was used to frequenting. It was all gleaming white décor, soft jazz and table service. He held the door open for me as we stepped inside. A cool breeze rushed through the place, signalling our arrival. I blushed, suddenly feeling quite out of place. The glances of the other patrons wreaked of snobbishness.

Once we'd been escorted to our seats I relaxed a little and wouldn't take no for an answer when I offered to buy the first round.

'No, seriously, you practically saved my life' I said emphatically, slapping my hand on the shiny surface of the table.

I nearly lost my balance on my high stool which tended to swivel at the slightest movement. The waiter who had up until this point seemed cool and disinterested, raised a curious eyebrow. James laughed as he gave in and allowed me to order him a cocktail. I ordered myself a glass of red wine. It wasn't my usual tipple but I didn't want to seem common by ordering a whiskey coke. Finding myself in austere, fancy surroundings, I heard my mother's words ringing in my ears; 'whiskey is an old man's drink.'

'So ah, how did you get involved with the communists?' James ventured, a gentle smile on his lips. 'I can't imagine your landlady approves of the company you're keeping.'

'No, she doesn't but we tend to avoid the topic' I said frowning slightly.

It was funny before but now it felt like a betrayal to talk about Barbara like this, as though confiding in me had also earned her my undying loyalty. Seeing my discomfort, James swiftly changed the subject and asked me how my studies were going.

'Oh, fine thanks' I said placidly.

The truth was amidst all my gallivanting, partying and drinking I'd almost forgotten the real reason I was in Bologna.

My academic standards had dramatically lowered in the time I'd been there but I'd resigned myself to being ok with just scraping a pass. I'd work hard in my final year to get that 2:1. But for now I was more interested in learning as much as I could about life beyond the realm of what was in my textbooks.

When our drinks arrived I eagerly took a generous gulp from my glass, almost downing the whole thing in one. Then I remembered my surroundings and felt a rush of embarrassment.

James smiled wryly before plucking the olive from the cocktail stick in his martini, tossing it in the air and catching it in his mouth. We once again drew attention from some of the other customers, but I didn't feel so self-conscious anymore.

'So, do you come here often?' I asked curiously. James didn't seem as out of place as I did but it still didn't quite seem like his scene.

'Nah, first time. A friend recommended it as a classy joint. I suppose I just wanted to impress you' he said with a sly grin.

I felt the heat rising to my cheeks and took another sip of my wine to steady myself. It was smooth and light and went down easily, almost too easily. I wasn't really a wine person, but that was by far the best I'd ever tasted. Not like the vinegary stuff I was used to drinking out of a box back at uni.

After that, the conversation flowed with ease. James told me some more about his roommates; the ones who had helped to save me that fateful night. Francesco, who I'd met at the squatter's building, was an artist originally from Naples who made wood carvings for a living and pedalled his wares on the streets of Bologna. James' eyes sparkled as he explained how beautiful his handiwork was. He'd even had his own stall at the Christmas markets.

I listened, somewhat enviously, never before imagining that such a bohemian lifestyle was actually possible. Absent-mindedly I dipped my finger in my wine and traced the rim of my glass, causing it to ring out a clear note.

'Hey that's a neat trick!' exclaimed James in wonder.

I stopped suddenly as a twinge of self-consciousness returned. James went on to tell me that he lived with two other guys; Giacomo, an authentic *Bolognese* who worked in a pub and Ben, a fellow American from New York who ran an online business selling stock imported from China.

'I don't really understand what he does, but I think he's pretty rich' said James matter-of-factly. 'He told me once that he made some good bitcoin investments a while back.'

I smiled amusedly. They sounded quite the motley crew, like the cast of a sitcom. I ventured to ask about James' family and learnt that he had a twin sister and three brothers.

'Yeah, Laura's pretty tough since she grew up fighting with three older brothers but me and her have that twin bond you know? We're like that' he said, crossing his fingers. 'I've always fought her corner.'

I felt a twinge of envy again, being reminded of my only child status. I'd always wondered what it would have been like to have an older sibling to look up to or a younger one upon whom I could impart my knowledge and wisdom, not that I had a lot of that…

'Can you sense what she's thinking or feeling even when you're apart…like telepathy?' I asked.

He laughed, running a hand through his thick chestnut hair.

'Yeah, I wouldn't say we're telepathic, but we do have some kind of sixth sense. Like if she was upset or in trouble I'd just feel it, ya know?'

'It must be hard for you to be apart' I said.

'Yeah, it was tough at first but we both agreed that we needed to spread our wings and live independent lives at some point' he said brightly, but a hint of sadness briefly flickered in his eyes.

Now it was my turn to swiftly change the subject. I prattled on a little bit about my hometown and the friends I'd made in Bologna. Then, buoyed up by wine, I ventured to lay my cards on the table.

'So, James, in case you hadn't noticed, I like you' I said, attempting a sultry smile as I bit my lip.

'Yeah, I know, you already told me, remember? *I think I love you*' he said, gesturing air quotation marks.

My face fell and I squirmed in discomfort which almost made me fall off my chair again. I'd completely forgotten about the text but hadn't had enough wine to block out my embarrassment.

'Oh god, oh god, oh god. I was really drunk, I don't even remember sending that, I…'

He cut me off by taking my hand in his across the table.

'Hey, don't sweat it, I don't care. I know you well enough by now to know that you're a bit unpredictable when you've had a few' he laughed.

'So…you don't think I'm a psycho? I asked tentatively.

'No Kerry, I don't think you're a psycho. Granted, you're not completely sane but hey, who is?'

I exhaled a sigh of relief. We ordered another round of drinks, laughed and chatted some more about diverse topics ranging from the weather in Chicago (which was quite similar to that of Bologna – really hot in summer, really cold in winter) to what superpowers we'd choose if we could. I'd go for the ability to fly so I could save money on plane tickets, but James said he'd rather be able to breathe under water since he was an avid snorkeller.

Feeling more at ease, I ventured to play footsie under the table. At first, I did it gently, so it could have passed as an accident. But then I grew bolder and pointedly brushed the inside of his shin with my ankle boot. James raised an eyebrow at glanced at me, intrigued, but didn't move away. Suddenly I noticed the time.

'Oh Shit' I said 'It's late. I'd better go home.'

It was a school night after all and I had an early morning lecture, plus I wanted to leave him wanting more. James looked disappointed but accepted that the evening was over. When we stepped back onto the street we were greeted by a blizzard. I wrapped my woollen coat tight around me as flecks of hail rained down on my face like needles. We stepped back briefly under the awning, supposing that it might ease off if we waited a while. Then James touched my arm and spoke softly in my ear.

'Do you want to come back to mine? I live closer to the centre than you do. You can wait it out there' he said.

Smooth. Well played James. Well played.

I returned his proposal with an impish grin and agreed. *So much for leaving him wanting more.* I knew right then that I wasn't going to make it to my morning lecture.

When we got back to James' flat, Francesco was still out and Giacomo was just leaving for his shift. He recognised me instantly.

'*Ciao bella*! You're still alive!' he said smiling as he passed me on the way out the door.

As we moved through to the living room I said a brief hello to the other American, Ben, who was watching TV while eating a bowl of cereal. Milk trickled down his chin as he talked. Like Francesco, he was also glad to see I wasn't dead. I felt embarrassed by the fact I couldn't remember my first meeting with either of them.

We paused briefly in the kitchen as James poured us each a glass of water and grabbed a bowl of olives.

'That's very Italian' I remarked.

'Yeah, well I'm not a completely ignorant American' he laughed.

James' room was quite a reasonable size. He left me alone while he went to the bathroom, so I snooped around a little, opening the odd drawer and perusing his bookshelf. He had a lot on Italian language as well as linguistics and English grammar. There was also a tank with a chameleon. His eyes swivelled so he was able to look in two opposite directions at once. I found it both fascinating and slightly unnerving. When James returned he caught me leafing through one of his cookery books.

'Hey, maybe I could make you dinner sometime' he said, sitting close to me on the bed so our bodies were only just touching.

'Yeah, I'd like that' I said as I smiled and put the book down.

'So, who's this guy?' I asked pointing to the chameleon.

'Oh, that's Karma' he said, 'You know, after that song by Boy George.'

I thought it was genius. He explained he'd adopted him from a guy who moved back to Australia and couldn't take him with him.

After a brief lull in our conversation I said, 'So, ah, this is a nice room.'

I'd reverted to small talk since the walk back in the cold had sobered me considerably, but I wasn't wrong. Soft furnishings, neat and tidy with everything in its place. A poster for the Chicago Bears football team was pinned to the back of the door. I popped an olive in my mouth and savoured its salty bitter taste.

I knew there was a natural order to things. He'd invited me to his place for one reason and one reason only. I was nervous. It wasn't like I hadn't had sex before. I had, *a lot*. But I was used to being a lot drunker and getting straight down to it in a messy and un-ceremonial fashion. In this case it seemed there would be preliminaries. I was both overwhelmed and excited by the prospect of a truly romantic sexual encounter; one I could fully remember and not regret the next day. James started to lightly run his fingers up and down my bare arm. I shivered involuntarily.

'Oh sorry, I didn't mean to' he stuttered.

'Oh no, it's fine' I assured, as I turned to face him properly. He'd hung his blazer over the door when we came in so was now just in a tight-fitting white t-shirt which teased at the promise of a beautifully sculpted specimen beneath. I gulped. *What if he didn't like my body? What if he thought I was fat? What if he's disgusted by my pubic hair?*

I was in the middle of another anxious thought when he leant over and kissed me. A soft, sensuous kiss which required minimum effort to keep the momentum going, like eating a Mr. Whippy. I ran a hand under his t-shirt and placed my palm flat on his chest, before moving it down to inspect his abs. My suspicions were delightfully confirmed. I peeled it off him to get a better look as his hands slid under my dress and around my back to fumble with my bra strap. I ended up having to do the honours myself. I don't know why guys even bother; bra fastenings are like Rubik's cubes to them.

With my breasts free from their constraints he was able to explore them with his hands, lightly cupping, kneading and pinching my nipples between his thumb and forefinger. I moaned into his mouth. This was good. When he tried to pull my dress over my head I stopped him suddenly.

'Oh, um, can we turn off the lights?' I asked, biting my lip.

'Ah yeah, sure, a bit of ambient lighting coming right up.'

He didn't really understand that I wanted to be in *complete* darkness but I settled for the soft glow of a bedside lamp over making my insecurities blatantly obvious. I glanced at the swell of his erection which was protruding through his boxers as he flicked the switch. I thought about how I'd like him to flick something else.

Once I'd completely undressed I gasped as James pinned me to the bed under the covers with just the right amount of force. He kissed me again, soft and hard and my vagina tingled in anticipation. I was wetter than an Irish summer. He politely asked me if I was ready and I nodded. Then he entered. I dug my nails into his back as he rocked back and forth on top of me. I moaned in delight and muttered involuntary words, like 'Fuck' and 'Oh Jesus'. I call it sextourettes.

'You're so beautiful' he whispered in my ear, his warm breath only serving to enhance my arousal.

My head swam with delight and visions of romance as I wondered if this would be more than a one-night stand. As he reached climax I wrapped my legs around his body. He came with a grunt and collapsed on top of me, spent with pleasure. I ran my fingers through his thick hair and breathed a sigh of content. After he'd withdrawn and discreetly disposed of the condom, he started kissing my breasts and then moving down the length of my body with his tongue. I stopped him before he reached my nether regions.

'Oh, sorry, I just thought, well you'd want to...' he said, looking up at me, slightly perplexed.

'Oh, it doesn't matter, I'm fine really' I said. It wasn't that I didn't want to orgasm as well. I did. But I hadn't shaved down there in weeks and I knew we'd end up in an embarrassing situation where he'd choke on my wiry hairs and I'd have to direct him as to how exactly I liked to be pleasured (because he definitely wouldn't be able to figure it out on his own) and I just didn't have the patience in that moment.

He came back up to lie beside me and we cuddled as I rested my head on his chest.

'You're good at that' he said, lightly brushing his fingers across my forearm.

'Thanks' I said smiling. I appreciated the compliment, but I didn't think sex was something that could really be ranked as a skill. Anyone can do it and for a woman, to excel simply requires a reasonable amount of hip thrusting, mild flexibility and the ability to lie on your back. We lay still in contented silence for a while before untangling ourselves so we were more comfortable and I wasn't cutting off the blood supply to James's left arm. After a bit of whispered pillow talk about chameleons and cats, we kissed each other goodnight and eventually drifted off to sleep.

***

A few nights later it was film night at Ronan and Marc's place, a tradition we'd started to do every Friday since Marc had stolen a projector from a uni store cupboard. All we needed was a big white sheet and some cushions on the floor to create our own home cinema. Marc had once told me that he didn't really watch films but it seemed living with Ronan had changed all that.

Tonight, we'd chosen to watch the latest Woody Allen creation. Ronan absolutely loved him as a director but I personally found his films confusing and headache inducing. But if Ronan was happy, I was happy. He didn't seem sad about his break-up with Rosie anymore and had hardly mentioned it lately.

He and Marc seemed to have grown a lot closer too since they'd been living together and regularly did things just the two of them, like trips to museums and nearby cities. I was glad, if albeit a little jealous.

I'd texted Anita and Ronan straight away to tell them about James and they'd been so excited about it all, bombarding me with loads of questions. It was slightly overwhelming, like being interrogated by the police, or at very least the *Polizia Municipale*.

'Is he good in bed?'

'Is he good craic?'

'When can we meet him?'

'Is he treating you right?'

This was the first time we'd had the opportunity to talk about it in person. Marc played the perfect host by getting everyone cups of tea whilst we got settled on the floor cushions. Ronan couldn't wait to spill the beans.

'Hey everyone, Kerry has a boyfriend!'

'Shushhh' I squealed, covering his mouth with my hand.

'It's only been a few days, keep your hair on!'

I blushed, turning the colour of the crimson cushions we were sitting on. The décor of Marc's apartment was very warm and Aladdin's cove-like with warm autumnal hues, dusty books and small curiosities like a silver pocketwatch arranged neatly above the mantlepiece. Tatiana had knitted them a throw for the sofa embroidered with golden leaves and red roses as a housewarming present.

'Come on now, no need to be embarrassed with us' said Anita as she playfully tickled my ribs.

Tatiana and Erik expressed their congratulations as well, beaming at me like proud parents. It was all a little bit hyperbolic, you'd have thought I'd announced our engagement already! Were my friends really that desperate for me to find love? Marc re-emerged from the kitchen carrying the teas on a small wooden tray. He smiled at me, so I knew he'd overheard. Part of me wanted him to be jealous, but not because I still liked him in a romantic way. I just felt foolish for how I'd acted.

During the film Ronan sat close to Marc on the sofa, periodically ruffling his hair and every so often Marc would whisper in Ronan's ear as though they were sharing a private joke.

After the film I left to go and work on my mural at the squatter's building. It was getting late, but the days were growing longer so a slither of daylight remained as I made my way through the familiar heavy iron door and up the steps to my designated wall space. As much as I enjoyed being a social butterfly, I also really valued alone time. I needed those moments by myself to breathe and recalibrate, to process whatever was going on for me and lately there had been a lot. Anita made a move to come with me and looked a little disappointed when I said I wanted to be alone. But I knew she understood.

It seemed I was the only person around. I lit a few candles (not wanting to run up the electricity bill) and got to work on my mural. I was working on a particular scene with two abstract Picasso-esque figures, one in tones of red holding a locket and the other in shades of blue holding a key. My mind calmed as I painted and in the soft glow of the candlelight it felt almost ritualistic. Then I heard a rattle coming from one of the rooms that adjoined the corridor. I froze. *Could it be a burglar?*

Armed with only a paintbrush and an ounce of bravery I crept toward the noise in order to investigate. When I flung open the door of the room in question I stifled a scream. It was just Omar, diligently working away by candlelight on his latest comic strip. *Fumetti* were very popular in Italy and Omar was an expert at crafting funny stories with charming characters and watercolour illustrations to accompany them.

'Oh God' I said, catching my breath. 'You really scared me.'

Omar, who'd barely reacted to my arrival, so engrossed was he in his work, now just looked up and smiled dreamily at me.

'Oh sorry, I didn't mean to startle you.'

He beckoned me over to come and review his latest piece of work, a comic about a woman who was half-human, half-cat and found herself in all sorts of embarrassing mishaps. As I read and looked at the drawings I started to wonder, is this about me? I didn't want to be egotistical, but the main character was called 'Kara' and she was constantly being followed around by a Fox-man who adored her from afar called 'Oban.' It was both flattering and unsettling at the same time. As though reading my mind, Omar took my hand in his and said softly, 'Don't you see Kerry, everyone's in love with you, you can see it in their eyes.'

I opened my mouth in surprise, not quite sure how to respond before making a hasty excuse to leave. Omar offered for me to sleep on the floor of the studio, saying he had some nice sleeping bags and a spare mattress, but I politely declined, opting instead to grab my things, and run down the steps two at a time. He didn't try to stop me and as I'd left I'd looked back to see him returning to his work as though nothing had happened. It was surreal.

When I arrived home Barbara was snoring in her usual spot on the sofa in front of the TV. The Italian X-factor was on with Mika hosting. I turned it off just as they were about to declare which contestants had gotten through to the next round and pulled a thin blanket over her to make her more comfortable. She'd been visiting the hospital a lot lately and it seemed like Marina didn't have long left but she was stubborn as an Ox so wasn't going without a fight. My heart ached for Barbara.

That night before I went to sleep I did something I hadn't done in a long time. I knelt by the edge of my bed and prayed. I'd grown up Catholic but as I got older and became conscious of all the evil in the world I'd stopped believing that the Universe was somehow governed by an all-powerful, all-seeing benevolent force. Now, after having experienced so much beauty and chaos, it didn't seem so fantastical. *God, if you have to take Marina home, please let her go peacefully and easily. And please send some angels to look after Barbara.*

Chapter 15

I woke up with a throbbing headache. My mouth tasted like a swamp. I groped for my phone to check the time. *Shit! Shit! double shit!*

I only had half an hour before I was due to meet James at the train station. The night before it had been St. Patrick's day so naturally the Emerald had hosted a big shindig. Ronan was working but since it was so busy he managed to get away with slipping me free whiskeys all night. My stomach lurched at the memory.

I'd slept with James a few more times since our first rendezvous and we'd been texting quite a bit, but we hadn't been on any more proper dates. I was beginning to wonder if I was only a casual fling to him. But then, just as I was losing hope he suggested a day trip; a clear sign of commitment.

Still, I couldn't decide whether a day out in Verona would be terribly romantic or spell doom for our relationship. Romeo and Juliet was, after all, Shakespeare's greatest tragedy. That's if I even managed to make it to the station on time. As I wiped away the residue of green eyeshadow, I cursed myself for agreeing to do anything on the 18th March. I should have known better. I didn't have time to shower so sprayed myself with copious amounts of perfume to mask the stench of alcohol and hastily jumped on my bike, still wearing the same clothes from the night before.

By the time I made it to the station I was sweating. Thankfully my forest green blouse was made from a forgiving light chiffon, so no dark patches had formed under my armpits. My phone had been buzzing non-stop in my pocket, most likely with anxious texts from James enquiring as to my whereabouts. I ran up to him panting, trying in vain to cough out my excuses.

'Come on! Where have you been?' he asked, slightly irritated.

He grabbed my wrist and dragged me through the crowd to the platform where we just about managed to jump aboard our train on time. Once in the comfort of the carriage, I breathed a sigh of relief. The red and terracotta shades of Bologna soon melted into lush greens as we passed rolling fields and vineyards, leaving the city behind. The sun was shining today, signalling the beginning of Spring.

'I'm sorry I was late, I...well... it was quite a heavy one last night' I said sheepishly, looking down at my hands.

'Hey, don't worry about it, you made it' said James with a smile, all trace of irritation now gone.

'I know what you Irish are like. In Chicago they dye the river green on St. Patrick's day and everyone goes crazy. You'd love it.'

'I'm sure I would' I replied.

Despite my pounding hangover I smiled back at him and for a brief moment all was right with the world.

We didn't talk much on the train, preferring to enjoy the view and one another's company in silence. This suited me since I was still sobering up, but we didn't yet know one another well enough for it to be a comfortable silence. At least from my point of view. My mind still whirred with anxious thoughts like *Oh God, does he think I'm really immature?*, *What if we actually don't have anything in common and it's all just about sex?*, *Is he too old for me?*, *Am I too young for him?*

At some point he pulled out a crossword book and some reading glasses and I enjoyed watching him bite his lip as he lingered on what I presumed was a particularly puzzling clue. He really was a fine specimen of a man, the kind you picture when someone is described as 'tall, dark and handsome.' It just all seemed too good to be true. A voice in the back of my mind gnawed, 'What's the catch?'

In the middle of the journey, I had to rush to the toilet to be sick. James gently knocked on the door to ask if I was ok. I assured him I was fine in between shame filled retching which wasn't helped by the rickety motion of the train. Afterwards I managed to sleep off a bit of my fuzzy headedness. When we arrived James gently shook me awake.

'Hey Kerry, we're here' he said, grinning wildly.

I yawned and hastily wiped a sliver of drool away from the corner of my mouth.

As we stepped out of the station, the midday sun was beating down on us, illuminating Verona in all its rustic charm and beauty. It felt like a betrayal of Bologna to admit my enrapture but enraptured I was, nonetheless.

The first thing we did was get a gelato. James had insisted on paying for my mint choc-chip ice cream and mostly everything we did that day for that matter. This time I let him. Feminist principles aside, I realised it didn't pay to have such pride when the fact remained that I was a student living off an Erasmus grant, and he was a working man.

Next, we visited the Roman amphitheatre with its strong impenetrable arches, where gladiators once fought to the death. Our tour guide, a stout and short young man with glasses called Enrico, regaled us with the history of the great arena in between popping mints from a bag he carried in the back pocket of his jeans. At the end, when James was busy chatting to some other Americans we'd met on the tour, I politely asked the guide if I could have one of his mints. I hadn't had time to brush my teeth that morning, plus I'd been sick on the train. Enrico graciously obliged but I had to brush him off when he asked for my number in return.

'*Ah capisco*, this is your *Innamorato*?' he said, gesturing to James who was deep in conversation with another guy from the US.

He looked to be around the same age, wearing the standard tourist uniform of backpack and baseball cap, and they were laughing and fist bumping as though they'd known one another for years.

'Hmmm, yes I suppose so' I said, somewhat unconvincingly.

I wasn't really sure what James and I were. *Boyfriend and girlfriend? Friends with benefits? Just friends? Did we want the same things? Did I even know what I wanted?*

Sensing my doubt, Enrico countered with a wink, 'Well *Signorina*, if you ever need a real man, you know, an Italian stallion, then you know where to find me.'

I stifled a laugh as I sucked on my mint and told him I'd bear that in mind.

As we were leaving I looked over my shoulder to see Enrico flexing his bicep and waving at me. I waved back as a reflex. James remained oblivious and we crossed over the main square, Piazza Brá, to enjoy an espresso and lunch on the outdoor terrace of a nearby restaurant.

'Gee, isn't it incredible to be surrounded by all of this history?' James said, as he delicately dabbed the corner of his mouth with a napkin.

'Yeah, definitely' I said, trying my best to stomach my food.

I still didn't feel myself, but I didn't want to throw up an expensive plate of traditional risotto. I poured myself some water from the jug James had thoughtfully ordered for the table and prayed to all the Gods that I wouldn't be sick.

'If you could be any historical figure for the day, who would you be?' I asked playfully, in an attempt to take my mind off the nausea.

'Hmm, gee, well that's a hard one' he replied, thoughtfully rubbing his chin. 'I'd have to say Shakespeare, I mean he was such a cool dude. Imagine having such talent for writing.'

'Oh wow, I didn't know you were a fan' I replied.

Speaking of which, I used a menu to waft some air over my flushed face. This garnered a few curious glances from an elderly couple at the opposite table since it wasn't a particularly hot day. I grimaced awkwardly at them before turning my attention back to James.

'Well as an English teacher it's hard not to be, he's had such an influence on our language' he said emphatically, whilst twirling some spaghetti round his fork.

'For example, did you know that so many words we say ubiquitously are from Shakespeare, like 'to be in pickle' was coined in The Tempest and the word 'addiction' didn't appear until the bard used it in Othello?'

I smiled. It was nice to see a man so passionate about something. Apathy was my biggest turn off.

'Now I know why you were so eager to come here' I said.

'Well yes, it's hard to resist the city that inspired such great works… and tales of love' he said as he reached across the table and took my hand.

I flinched, snatching it back. If I'd been drunk I wouldn't have cared but in the cold sober light of day I found public displays of affection, even minor ones like handholding, utterly abhorrent. I could tell James felt hurt, a flicker of disappointment in his eyes, but he did his best not to show it and promptly changed the subject.

Juliet's balcony was *the* main tourist attraction in Verona. I did my best to seem more enthusiastic about it than I felt since I didn't want James to think I'd gone off him or was averse to romance. But in all honesty it seemed like a waste of money to me. After all, there was very little conclusive evidence to suggest that Romeo and Juliet were even based on real people in history and the balcony everyone was clamouring to stand on wasn't even dated from that period. One blessing was that the queue wasn't too long since it wasn't peak season. When it was our turn to take a photo opportunity on the balcony I spread my arms wide and called out over the railings, 'Romeo, Romeo, where for art thou Romeo?'

I thought this would be funny and elicit a laugh, or at the very least a smile from James. But he just took the photo hastily on his phone and then looked at his feet, mumbling something about the fact that other people were waiting in line. I shuffled awkwardly back towards him, the redness returning to my cheeks.

One rough stone wall of Juliet's house is plastered with notes of all sizes and colours; love letters and pleas for guidance on matters of the heart. Some are crumpled and wedged in between the bricks, others are posted proudly for all to see. The effect is quite pretty really, a patchwork of fan mail for a fictional character. For modern-day purposes there are also some computers set up where one can email Juliet and ask for romantic advice. I didn't see the point of writing to a literary ghost, and it wasn't even a given that the 'Secretaries of Juliet' (the real people who responded to the letters) would reply to me, but whilst I was waiting for James to go to the toilet I hastily typed a message and hit 'Send' before I could change my mind.

As we meandered through the city James would periodically attempt to hold my hand. The most I could tolerate was a light finger brush before I'd feign ignorance and pretend that the hand in question was urgently needed elsewhere, to scratch my head or point at something interesting in the near distance, like a statue (of which there were many) or a cat (of which there were decidedly less). James wasn't as enamoured as I with the pudgy ginger Tom who I stopped to pet outside a fishmongers, but he waited patiently as the cat purred and greeted me by rubbing against my bare ankles.

In the historic centre we weaved in and out of shops selling leather handbags, jewellery, hand blown Murano glass sculptures from Venice, intricately carved wooden boxes and all manner of trinkets. I paused in a window to gaze upon a beautiful pendant, a garnet heart set in silver that glinted in the sunlight.

I would have bought it for myself, but I reasoned that the price tag exceeded what I could justify spending my grant on, at least until I received my next instalment. James bought some fridge magnets and postcards which I thought were a bit tacky, but I nodded and enthusiastically agreed that his siblings and friends back home would indeed love them.

As the sun was setting we made our way to the top of a hill for a panoramic view of the city. The terracotta roofed buildings below became bathed in an amber glow and the Adige river sparkled as the last light drained from the sky.

James put his arm around me, and I rested my head on his shoulder, partly because I was exhausted from the hike up the hill but also because I was feeling a sense of comfort and ease in his presence that hadn't been there earlier in the day. I even permitted him to hold my hand. The spot we were in was fairly secluded, so it didn't seem so embarrassing.

'Was our day trip everything you'd hoped it would be?', I asked dreamily as he gently tickled my palm with his thumb.

He looked me in the eyes, his dark pupils dilating within their hazel pools and held my gaze for a moment before replying softly, 'Yes, it has. Everything and more.'

We smiled at each other, and a contented sigh escaped my lips. Perhaps I had nothing to worry about after all?

Chapter 16

As well as painting my mural at the squatters' building I'd also been dabbling in some artwork at home. I decided to make something for Barbara's sick friend, in an attempt to lift her spirits.

'Ah È Bellissima!' Barbara exclaimed with glee when I showed her my finished creation. It was an abstract interpretation of Bologna, in different shades of acrylic paint. Russet, amber and gold shapes formed the skyline of the city I'd come to know and love, set against a cerulean sky with a shimmering rainbow. I'd also added in the serene figure of an angel, perched atop San Petronio cathedral, smiling serenely down at the people-less streets below.

'Marina will love it' she assured me.

As she gripped my hand across the breakfast table I could tell she was holding back tears. When I carefully covered the canvas in pink tissue paper so Barbara could take it on her next visit to the hospital, it struck me that the wrapping was as delicate as life itself.

***

Things were going reasonably well with James. Our day in Verona seemed to have been the gateway into a more serious relationship and we'd been seeing more and more of one another. I'd accompanied him on a trip to the opera during which I'd dozed off in the middle of a performance of Puccini's Madame Butterfly. It wasn't that the opera was particularly boring, I'd just been up since the crack of dawn that day so I could hastily finish an essay on Italian linguistics before the deadline. I'd awoken with a start as James jabbed me in the ribs. He said I'd started to snore, a look of both amusement and mild embarrassment on his face. I whispered my apology in the dark theatre as a tall thin Italian woman behind us sharply ordered me to 'shush.'

I'd also been round to watch some American Football with him and Ben, his New yorker flatmate, which he streamed online from his laptop. I didn't really have any clue what was going on and the sport completely baffled me despite James' patient attempts to explain the rules. All I knew was that James supported the Chicago Bears and Ben was a New York Giants fan and whenever someone scored they went mad, jumping up and thumping their chests like deranged apes. James, who was normally quite a quiet and reserved person seemed to transform into an utter maniac when it came to sports and Ben was no different. Eventually I gave up trying to pretend I was interested and started bringing a book to these occasions which I read absent mindedly over the din of their clinking beer bottles and wild cheering.

When it came to sex our lovemaking had fallen into quite a predictable and monotonous pattern whereby we took it in turns to be on top and I gave up any hope of having an orgasm. It was my own fault really. The first time we slept together I said it didn't matter because I didn't want to put too much pressure on him, but I didn't mean that it didn't matter *ever.* It's not that James was inherently selfish or anything. Outside of the bedroom he was the kindest and most generous person I'd ever met, constantly surprising me with bouquets of yellow carnations or tickets to an outdoor concert. But when we were in bed together it now just felt like we were going through the motions, and I didn't know how to broach the sensitive topic of 'spicing things up.'

'Are you sure this is the guy for you Kerry?' asked Anita bluntly, cutting me off mid-sentence as I explained the situation between James and I.

We were standing outside the main university library and after being inside its dark mahogany interior, the sun was blinding. End of year exams were looming, so we'd been teaming up to study together, but our sessions were always interspersed with smoke breaks (for Anita) and trips to get gelato (for me) whilst we discussed the meaning of life and who we thought was going to win the Italian X factor, so I'm not entirely sure how productive they really were. Anita regarded me impatiently as she puffed smoke from her cigarette upwards like a sexy dragon. Her hair was piled roughly on top of her head in a messy bun and a pen nestled comfortably behind her left ear.

I sighed. She always knew when I was lying, could see right through my lies as though they were water. But that didn't stop me from trying.

'Well, does anyone really know who the 'right' person is for them?' I replied. 'Surely it's all just a case of trial and error and figuring things out. I don't think we've had enough time yet to really ascertain...'

'Do you love him?' she asked suddenly, her question slicing through my ramblings like a knife.

Her directness startled me so much that I took a clumsy step backwards and nearly fell over. She reached over to steady me, a soft hand gripping my shoulder as the scent of her perfume, some blend of clementine and magnolia, filled my nostrils.

I thought I did. But maybe it was just infatuation? Lust? Adrenaline and dopamine from a scenario that was always just destined to be a year-abroad romance? Something I could write about in my diaries to reminisce about years later when I was grey and wise.

'Uh, sure. I suppose so' I said rather unconvincingly. Anita smirked but didn't challenge me any further.

'Come on' she said as she stubbed her cigarette out on the pavement with one of her canary yellow converse.

'We've got work to do.'

As she dragged me back into the cool darkness of the library I felt a shiver of doubt run down my spine.

***

A few days later Tatiana had convinced me to invite James on a double date with her and Erik.

'Oh, it will be so fun!' she'd squealed as she pirouetted around Neptune's fountain, barefoot and nimble.

It was around 3am following a night out, we'd just had a slice of hot, thin and crispy pizza and everything seemed magical under the star-lit sky. Of course I'd agreed.

Now as I found myself at James' school, all set to surprise him at his place of work, I wondered if this really was the romantic gesture I'd intended or just weird and stalkerish. I asked where I could find him at the front desk and they directed me to his classroom immediately, without even pausing to ask who I was or why I was there.

I sheepishly knocked before I entered and found James in full flow, gesticulating at verb tables for the future tense on the board. A projector softly hummed, and the scratching of pens on paper abruptly stopped when I entered. The students all turned to look at me in unison. James mainly taught adults but this was a class comprised solely of teenage boys who needed a bit of extra tuition during the Easter holidays. James stopped talking too and looked at me with an expression that combined shock and curiosity with just a hint of embarrassment.

'Uh James, can I speak to you for a moment?' I asked, gesturing to the corridor.

'Um, yeah, sure. Just a sec' he said as he hurriedly ordered some papers on his desk and gave instructions to the class to read a certain page of their textbooks while he was gone.

One boy boldy piped up, 'Sir is that your girlfriend?' which elicited a chorus of 'Ooohs' from the other boys.

James blushed slightly but simply ordered the class to be quiet before he slipped out to join me in the corridor. I found his authoritative tone quite arousing.

'Hey Kerry, to what do I owe this pleasant surprise?' he said, seeming only mildly flustered.

'Oh, I'm sorry, I didn't mean to disturb you, I thought you might be on your lunch break' I said.

'Oh, shucks I'm sorry' he said whilst rubbing the back of his neck. 'I would offer to take you for lunch, but we've just done a test so I'm going to be spending my break today marking.'

'Oh, it's ok, no worries. Um, would you fancy coming on a double date with me tonight?'

'Uh, sure' he said with a hint of surprise.

He hadn't met any of my friends yet and I'd sort of intentionally been keeping it that way despite his insistence that he wanted to be introduced. I didn't want their opinions and judgments just yet. But I wasn't so close to Tatiana and Erik so my hope was they wouldn't scrutinise our compatibility as closely as Anita or Ronan might have.

'Great' I beamed. 'Meet you at Osteria dell'Orsa at seven.'

'And if you wear this suit, dessert will definitely be on the menu' I said as I suggestively pulled him closer to me by his navy blue tie.

He opened his mouth as though to reply but seemed stunned into silence. At this point a raucous shouting had erupted from inside the classroom.

'Ah got to go, see you later' he said before pecking me on the cheek and hurriedly returning to his class.

I heard him shouting 'Silence!' as I merrily skipped down the corridor, hopeful for the evening which lay ahead.

***

The restaurant was nestled in a charming corner of the university district. When I arrived, I peered through the window to see Erik and Tatiana already seated at the table, fawning over one another as usual. The glow of candles in an array of coloured glass jars illuminated the crisp white tablecloths as Tatiana daintily fed Erik morsels of crusty bread dipped in olive oil and balsamic vinegar. I checked the time on my phone. For once I'd managed not to be late, but it was only because I'd cycled at a record pace. When I turned around James suddenly appeared, smiling warmly at me. He was wearing a salmon pink shirt with chocolate brown trousers and a tie to match. To me he looked like a sexy professor. At any rate, he was certainly sexier than any of my *actual* professors.

'Shall we go in? After you' he said as he held the door open for me.

When I stepped through the door he gently rested his hand on the small of my back which sent a shiver of pleasure through my body.

We made the usual introductions and small talk during the ordering of drinks and antipasti, which although tedious and boring, seemed to be the done thing on such occasions.

I could tell Tatiana approved of James. She kept looking over and grinning at me knowingly between sips of white wine. James and Erik immediately found common ground, both being avid sports fans. Even though volleyball and American football are completely different, they both seemed genuinely interested in the other's game. Tatiana pulled me to the toilets for a girly tête-a-tête in between the starter and main course, leaving the boys engrossed in their conversation.

'Wow, you've done well my dear' she said as she reapplied her baby pink lipstick in the mirror. 'Your boyfriend is so handsome and sweet, I'm so happy for you.'

She turned around to lovingly tuck a stray strand of hair behind my ear, a gesture that seemed almost motherly.

'Thanks Tatiana, but um, I don't think I can officially say he's my boyfriend. We haven't really discussed it.'

She frowned, pulling out a compact powder case and proceeding to top up her already immaculate face of make-up.

'Well, what are you waiting for? Just ask him already! He's cute and kind, you're beautiful and smart, you're meant to be together. Make it official!'

I sighed as I looked down at my purple faux-leather ankle boots and played with the fabric of my black chiffon dress.

'It just never seems to be the right time. I don't want to make things weird' I confessed.

This was the longest relationship I'd ever had and I didn't want to mess it up by seeming over eager or clingy. Couldn't things just be allowed to evolve and bloom as they may without the labels?

As though she'd read my mind Tatiana replied, 'No, don't be ridiculous. It's been months! If he's not willing to call himself your boyfriend now, he never will be. You don't want to be wasting your precious time on someone who's not worth it. I know you care deeply about him Kerry, I see the twinkle in your eyes when you look at him, don't listen to what Anita says...' She put her hand to her mouth suddenly, realising she'd said to much.

'Why, what does Anita say?' I asked, raising at eyebrow at her reflection in the mirror.

'Oh nothing, forget it. I shouldn't have said anything. She just worries about you that's all' she said as she hastily teased out her soft blond hair with her fingers before shooing me out of the bathroom in front of her.

When we sat back down Erik and James were still chatting like old friends who'd known one another for years.

'Hey Kerry, this guy is an absolute gem, hang on to this one' said Erik as he raised his beer. 'Great taste in beer as well, that's how you know he's a good man.'

James bit his lip, a signal of discomfort I'd come to recognise, but he quickly brushed aside any signs of unease by smiling and calling over the waiter to order dessert. Tatiana noticed too though and shot me a look that said as much.

'So um, Kerry tells me you guys are engaged. Any date set for the wedding?' asked James, swiftly changing the subject.

I reached out to hold his hand under the table. He didn't resist but his palm was uncharacteristically sweaty.

'Oh well we're still so young' said Tatiana dreamily, her head resting on Erik's shoulder. 'We want to have fun and travel before that and of course we have to finish our studies so no date yet, but we do know we want to spend the rest of our lives together.'

Erik concurred by stroking her hair affectionately.

'Yes we don't know what the future will hold, we both have dreams, but I'm sure everything will be fine as long as we're together' he said.

I took a generous gulp of my red wine as I felt a familiar stirring of jealousy in the pit of my stomach. I realised now it wasn't particularly their relationship or love that I envied. It was their *certainty.* It seemed that from the moment they'd met on the beach at Ravenna they knew they were meant for one another and that was it.

Meanwhile I was a walking bag of fear, anxiety and doubt in all romantic matters. Most of my dating experience thus far had been comprised of first dates and one-night stands and although such experiences were hollow and unfulfilling at least I knew what was going to happen. The formula was simple and followed a predictable pattern whereas the longer a relationship progressed, the more unforeseen variables there were.

'Hey Kerry, you're hurting me' James whispered in my ear, pulling me out of my inner monologue.

I spluttered out an apology, not realising I'd been gripping his hand so tightly. I ordered another bottle of wine for the table but ended up drinking most of it myself.

By the time we were polishing off our panna cotta it was late. James got the bill and helped me put on my jacket before we left. We'd decided to go on to a bar afterwards and Tatiana and I once again found ourselves alone, choosing to wait on the street as the guys went to visit an ATM.

'Ooh look, delicious' she said, peering through the window of a now closed bakery and delighting at the rows of cakes and stuffed pastries with their joyful decorations. I couldn't fathom how she managed to maintain her slender figure whilst being such an avid lover of food.

'So, uh, come on, what did Anita say?' I asked, trying to reprise our earlier conversation even though my words were now a little slurred. Tatiana sighed and put her arm around me.

'Nothing. She was just worried that you were wasting your time on a guy who didn't deserve you. And now, well, I wonder if she's right.'

I didn't say anything in reply. The wine from earlier now seemed to be activating the depression switch as a feeling of sadness took hold.

'Can I ask you something' I said meekly, tears forming in my eyes.

'Sure honey, anything' she replied tenderly.

'How did you know Erik was the one?'

'I just did.'

'But I mean, how does he compare to other guys you've dated. How do you know one of them might have been the one if you'd given them a little more time?'

She mulled this over for a second, lightly chewing the inside of her cheek.

'Well Kerry, I haven't been very lucky in love in the past. All of my exes cheated on me and the last one used to beat the shit out of me. The bruises have faded but I'll never forget it. I grew up watching my father treat my mother like that, so I thought it was normal.'

Her voice was unwavering as my eyes widened in shock. I always saw her as some magical fae-like being who just exuded joy and happiness, oblivious to the perils of this world, so it was hard to fathom that she'd been through such hardship.

'Honestly, I was scared to open up to love again. I closed off my heart because I didn't want to get hurt but when I met Erik I just knew, something was different. It's hard to describe but I just knew he wasn't like the others, that I'd be safe with him. But it's more than just a feeling of being safe. It's like I've come home, I can be myself, I don't have to hide anymore. That to me is what real love is.'

I nodded and hugged her tight, letting my tears seep into her sweet-smelling hair.

'I'm so happy for you Tatiana, so happy. You deserve to be happy. You deserve it all.'

As she pulled me back and looked me in the eyes, I saw a strength and courage in her beautiful bone structure that had previously passed me by.

'And so do you my darling. You deserve to be happy just as much as the rest of us. Never settle for less than the best' she said, as she lovingly wiped away my tears and fixed my streaky mascara with a tissue she materialised from her handbag.

'But for now, let's go and do some shots.'

I smiled and nodded in agreement as we skipped down the street to reunite with our men.

Chapter 17

The next morning, I woke up with a pounding headache. James was sitting next to me holding a freshly brewed espresso.

'Hey there sleepy head, I wondered if you were ever going to wake up' he said, gently rubbing my back.

I looked over at Karma, the chameleon, to see him judging me with one beady eye whilst the other revolved in its socket, fixing itself on the target of a fly that had foolishly ventured into his tank.

'Wh- what happened?' I asked tentatively as I eagerly took the proffered coffee and downed it in one gulp. I couldn't remember much past the first bar we'd visited after dinner, but I sensed we'd been to more.

'Well let's just say it's not the first time I've had to carry out of a bar.' He smirked at me, and I winced in embarrassment.

'Hey, don't worry about it' he said quickly, sensing my shame. 'Fancy breakfast?'

It was a sunny Sunday morning, so we sauntered down to Giardini Margherita where there was a quaint little café nestled in between tall pine trees at the end of a long pond. I was surprised to see some terrapins by the water, lazily sunning themselves on the rocks.

As I was digging into my omelette James took a small black box tied with a red ribbon out of his jacket pocket.

'Here, I have something for you' he said, placing it in front of me on the table.

'Oh wow, thanks, what's this for?'

'Think of it as a very late birthday present' he said with a smile that melted my heart. I really did want things to work out between us, more than anything. But the gnawing doubt remained.

I opened it eagerly to discover a beautiful pendant, a garnet heart set in silver.

'Wait, is this the same one that I was looking at in Verona? How? I didn't think you'd even noticed me looking at it?'

I was genuinely touched. It was such a thoughtful gift.

'I saw how much you loved it and I know it's your birthstone, so I made another trip a couple of weeks ago to get it for you. I'm glad you like it.'

I immediately put it on, admiring how the bright red gemstone caught the light, giving the illusion that there was a small fire burning on my decolletage.

'It suits you' he said, before he seemed to stare off into the distance, a hint of sadness in his voice.

'I love it' I replied, beaming happily back at him, choosing to pretend that nothing was wrong.

We sat for a while, watching sparrows flitting across the pond as the wind blew softly through the trees. A waitress came and cleared away our plates. I anxiously fiddled with my new pendant. Eventually James broke the silence.

'Hey, listen Kerry, you know how you're going back to the UK soon?'

'Yes' I replied tentatively. I'm not sure if three months, could be strictly classed as 'soon.'

I hadn't really wanted to think about it. I didn't like where this was going.

'Yeah well do you think it's going to work out, you know, me and you. *Us*?'

He bit his lip and looked down, fidgeting with his hands in his lap.

'Yeah of course', I replied brightly. But I was fooling myself. A dark cloud of realisation dawned on me.

'Why, do *you* not think it's going to work out?'

He didn't say anything, still staring at his lap. I couldn't believe this was happening.

'You're breaking up with me aren't you', I whispered.

He nodded solemnly. I couldn't believe how much of a coward he was. He couldn't even bring himself to say it. The shock lodged in my throat. Then I burst into uncontrollable tears. True, we'd only been together for a few months but in the microcosm of Bologna, in such a beautiful, romantic city, it had seemed so intense, so real. Now I knew why we'd never made it official, why he didn't call me his girlfriend, why every time I'd tried to talk about the future he changed the subject.

'Hey Kerry, babe it's ok' he said, reaching for my hand across the table, a look of abject remorse in his eyes. I snatched my hand away, glaring back at him through my tears.

'And what's this then, my consolation prize?' I said vehemently, gesturing to my gift.

'No, it's not like that, Kerry...'

I got up and turned my back on him, marching furiously off the café's veranda and back out into the park. I couldn't decide what I was most angry about; the fact that he was splitting up with me or that he'd seen me cry. I hated crying in front of people.

'Hey wait' he said, rather unconvincingly.

He grabbed my arm, but I batted him away. I didn't need his pity.

'Don't fucking touch me' I hissed.

'Jeez Kerry, don't be like...'

'Don't be like what?' I snapped. *What did he expect me to be like?*

His eyes shifted around nervously. We were attracting some attention from people out enjoying their day of rest. *I'll make a scene if I want to. Let them look. What do I care?*

'Look I never meant for you to get hurt, it's not you it's me' he said.

I laughed wryly at his lack of originality.

'Go to hell!' I screamed, before dashing across a bridge that stretched over the water.

I managed to climb a tree that had some low branches and sat in it for what seemed like ages, crying and berating myself for choosing to ignore the signs. Perhaps James and I's romance had always been doomed to fail, nothing more than an extended holiday fling? I took off my necklace and threw it to the ground. Did he think he could bribe me into not being heartbroken? That this would make it any easier?

After a while my bum was getting sore from sitting on the rough bark. I rang Anita and she came as soon as she could, armed with tissues and a bottle of Bailey's.

'Come down from there, you're going to hurt yourself!' She called up at me.

I clambered down, narrowly avoiding being dive bombed by a Magpie which swooped close to my head. Anita suppressed a laugh which in turn made me laugh too even though my face was still wet with tears. We sat chatting for a while on the grass, drinking Bailey's in between hugging and listening to the coo of pigeons and the rustle of squirrels.

'Do you think he was really the one for you Kerry?' said Anita finally in her characteristic blunt fashion.

I sighed. 'I suppose not.'

She grinned. 'Well then, what's all this crying about?'

Before we left, I picked up my garnet necklace from the undergrowth. I may not have liked the motives behind it, but I still loved it and decided I didn't want to part with it just yet.

***

A few weeks later we were all deep in study mode as our final year exams were imminent. I buried myself in books and essays to take my mind off James. Anita remained my trusty study partner, often sitting with me to pull all-nighters in an attempt to cram our heads with knowledge before an exam the next day. It probably wasn't the best tactic to go into a test feeling wired and sleep deprived but it seemed to work for us.

When we had our study breaks I made a concentrated effort not to talk about James. I didn't want to become mopey and boring. Anita and I weren't too worried about the exams, both having the philosophy that a pass was enough. Ronan on the other hand was so stressed out that he almost forget it was his birthday. He reluctantly agreed to have a party but only after Anita practically begged him.

'Alright, but nothing too wild' he'd said as he peered at us over the piles of books and papers strewn on his living room floor. 'I mean it.'

***

One Saturday in May I decided to go for a bike ride on my own, leaving the city behind and venturing into the surrounding verdant countryside. I managed to get as far as Sasso Marconi, the little town named after the scientist Guglielmo Marconi who invented the radio. It was so quiet and peaceful compared to Bologna which was always so bustling and vibrant. Pastel coloured buildings and clean white streets made it seem almost like a toy village.

Stumbling across a quaint little church called San Lorenzo, I left my bike outside and tiptoed inside. My eye was drawn straight away to a curious mechanical nativity scene with intricately painted and sculpted figures. It was amazing. It wasn't just the manger scene either. A whole miniature village had been created complete with stone buildings and shepherds warming themselves by a fire. I marvelled at how long and painstaking it must have been to create, how many hours of loving dedication had gone into making it.

My trainers squeaked against the shiny polished parquet floor as I chose a pew. I made the sign of the cross whilst looking at the large gold crucifix above the altar before kneeling down. I was the only person there. A rare feeling of peace and serenity cocooned me as my thoughts roamed freely.

Barbara was now practically living at the hospital as it had become apparent that Marina was in her final days. I did what I could to help, like reminding her to eat and doing more than my share of the cleaning and laundry but it still never quite felt like enough. One of my biggest fears was that when all was said and done I wasn't a very good person.

I found it difficult to measure my own morality and whilst I made a concentrated effort to live by a certain code of ethics, I constantly felt like I was falling short of the mark. But maybe that was the point? If we all went around thinking we were perfect upstanding citizens then there wouldn't be any room for improvement, would there?

My time in Bologna was coming to an end and whilst on one hand I felt like I'd learnt a lot, both in the academic sense and about myself, another part of me felt I'd squandered the whole experience, that I should have done more, been *more.* But perhaps that was just my ego talking again.

I'd made some wonderful friends, but I feared that they'd all vanish once I left Italy, that they were simply mirages I'd somehow conjured up in my mind. Despite our drunken promises to one another that we'd be friends forever and always stay in touch, I knew that life could be unexpected and nothing could be taken for granted. As I sat alone in the church I prayed.

God, I know I haven't always said or done the right thing but I'm trying my best. Thank you for all of this, for enabling me to come to Italy and meet so many wonderful people and have all of these amazing experiences.

I'm so grateful. Please show me how to be a good person, or at least help me to be a little bit better tomorrow than I was today. And if the love of my life is out there somewhere, please grant me the possibility of meeting them some day. Amen.

Chapter 18

It turned out that around the same time as Ronan's birthday there was also a big dance festival taking place in the city. Everywhere I looked there were people in flamboyant and glittery costumes, tights and spandex, showcasing every style from breakdancing to ballet. It seemed there was a flashmob waiting around every corner.

We'd agreed to have a quiet dinner in a quaint little trattoria of Ronan's choosing before ambling around the streets to enjoy the festival. He smiled and thanked us as we exchanged our gifts with him across the gingham tablecloth.

'Oh wow, this is amazing, thanks K-dog' Ronan enthused as he unwrapped a director's cut special edition DVD copy of his favourite film Everyone Says I Love You.

Erik and Tatiana got him tickets to the film festival happening the following year in Bologna.

'So, you'll have a reason to come back' said Tatiana sweetly.

We'd briefly discussed the idea of having a yearly reunion in Bologna or some other city once we'd parted ways. I hoped that would be the case. In Rome it was said if you threw a coin in the Trevi fountain then it meant you'd return. No such tradition existed in Bologna, but I'd thrown a few euros in Neptune's fountain anyway just in case.

Anita's gift was a lovely silk shirt with a marbled pattern in shades of blue and turquoise. His eyes glistened as he received it, and he thanked her profusely.

Marc was sitting by Ronan's side as was now the norm. He said he'd give Ronan his present later with a knowing glance at which Ronan blushed and hurriedly encouraged us all to order.

'Come on, I'm starving' he said, briskly handing us all a menu.

Our waiter for the evening was a plump mustachioed man whose eyes lit up when we told him it was Ronan's birthday. He clicked his fingers and soon it seemed we were enjoying unlimited wine, with the two carafes on the table constantly being refilled.

Even though our stomachs were lined with copious amounts of bread, pasta and pizza (the holy trinity of carbs) it wasn't long before we were all considerably drunk.

Erik and Tatiana started snogging with a reasonable amount of heavy petting that was definitely inappropriate for the establishment we were in. But they didn't seem to care.

'Oi, pour a glass of water over them two would you, someone' joked Ronan.

In my inebriated state I took this order literally and poured a nearby glass of water on the fornicating couple, causing them to yelp in shock.

'What the hell Kerry?' said Erik as he dabbed his face with a white fabric napkin and handed one to Tatiana so she could do the same.

Ronan laughed so much he nearly fell off his chair. It turned out that after a bit too much wine, laughter can be quite infectious and soon we became so raucous that we were politely asked to vacate the premises.

'Right O, better head home then' said Ronan cheerily as he staggered down the street with Marc.

'Nooo, come on' I pleaded. 'Stay out a bit longer. We haven't even seen the dancing. Just one more drink. Pleeeease.'

I swayed precariously as Anita suddenly swept me away and made an attempt to waltz with me. She laughed as I kept stepping on her toes.

'Yes come on Ronan' she chimed in. 'You're only 21 once for God's sake.'

Reluctantly he gave in to our pleas and soon we were marvelling at a demonstration of Bollywood dancing in Piazza Maggiore. The Indian performers moved in time to scintillating music as their sequined costumes dazzled, giving them the appearance of a shoal of tropical fish. Anita and I tried to copy what they were doing but we just kept falling over and bumping into nearby spectators which earnt us a lot of disgruntled exclamations and dirty looks.

Tatiana and Erik didn't stay out long. I figured they'd gone to have their own sort of party since they couldn't seem to keep their hands off one another.

We saw some more impressive performances of tap dancing, ballet and cha cha as we wandered around the city's streets but after a while all of the movement sort of blurred into one and I couldn't really appreciate it.

The four of us ended up back in the Lord Lister. It was a Europop night, so Marc rolled his eyes as Ronan dragged him onto the dancefloor, but he didn't resist. A glittering disco ball reflected all the colours of the rainbow upon us and the other revellers. Anita twirled me round to a song called Heroes, which had been the winning Eurovision entry for Sweden that year.

We are the heroes of our time, woah, woah....

I felt dizzy as I looked over to see Ronan and Marc holding hands and dancing like they were the only two people in the room.

But we're dancing with the demons in our minds...

Without thinking (alcohol removed that ability) I weaved over to them and shouted in Ronan's ear so he could hear me over the music.

'Hey, are you two guys a couple?'

'Uh, just leave it alone Kerry, for once yeah?' he said, shaking me off.

'No go on, you can tell me' I insisted not taking a hint.

'Hey, I don't mind if you two are gay for each other. Maybe we could have a threesome' I shouted in Marc's ear.

He recoiled back in shock and pushed me away.

'Fuck off Kerry, leave us alone' he shouted over the din of the club.

'Hey, it's alright, I don't mind if you two are bumming each other' I slurred.

Anita came over to see what all the fuss was about. Oblivious to the fact that Ronan was now crying and following Marc out to the smoking area, I pulled her over to the bar with me and promptly ordered us some tequila shots.

'Hey Kerry, maybe you should take it a bit easier' she said whilst gently touching my hand after we'd completed the well-known ritual of salt, shot and lime. 'I think you've had enough now.'

I swatted away her concerns like flies and proceeded to order two more shots. The last thing I remembered was waiting for a taxi barefoot by the side of the road.

***

The next morning, I woke up bleary eyed with a hangover to end all hangovers. My phone buzzed me awake. There was a text from Anita.

'I can't believe what you did. Don't EVER talk to me again.'

But what did I do? I frantically tried to search my memories for what despicable act she could be referring to but all I could draw were blanks. I flinched as something moved next to me in bed and then I realised that I wasn't in my usual blue room. The air reeked of sweat and booze and a tall pale man was lying next to me. All I could see was his slightly spotty back, and greasy jet-black hair. Tentatively I started to make a move, trying my best to gather my things and get out of there before he woke up. I was horrified to realise that I wasn't wearing any underwear. I felt sick.

I hastily got dressed which wasn't easy since I had to pick out my clothes from the pile that was strewn all over the floor. I did my best to tiptoe past the sleeping stranger, but I tripped on an empty bottle of vodka and plummeted to the floor causing him to jolt awake.

'Bloody hell K-dog, go easy, I'm trying to sleep here' said a familiar posh voice I'd recognise anywhere.

I turned around in horror to see Edward smirking at me, one hand propping up his smug face. I was momentarily lost for words. At least I now knew why Anita was so angry with me.

'Uh, did we, uh, you know…?'

I gulped, fearing I already knew the answer.

'Oh yeah, absolutely' said Edward proudly. 'You were well up for it.'

'Uh, I…I don't remember… what about Kristina?'

'What about her?' he said haughtily. 'She knows I sleep around, and she doesn't care. Polish girls are easy like that.'

I was so enraged, upset and confused at the same time and my head was pounding. Part of me wanted to ask him some more questions, to try and fill in the blanks in my memory but I knew that if I didn't get away from him soon I'd likely go to prison for murder.

'Fuck you Edward' I spat before swiftly exiting the bedroom, slamming the door as I went.

***

When I staggered through the front door of Barbara's flat all the blinds were drawn which was unusual since it was nearly midday. I fumbled around in the dark kitchen for a glass of water, eager to rehydrate and wash away the taste of alcohol and regret. It was only as I passed the living room that I noticed Barbara was still at home, lying under her duvet and staring blankly at the TV. It wasn't switched on. I didn't really want her to see me in my current state, but I wanted to know what was wrong, so I gently walked over and put a hand on her shoulder.

'Hey Barabara' I said softly, 'Are you off work today?'

She slowly turned to look at me. Her eyes were red and puffy. It seemed she'd been crying for hours and now had no more tears left. Gripping my hands in hers she simply said, 'Marina's gone.'

Chapter 19

A few days later I went round to Ronan and Marc's place the next day to apologise and see if I could make any more sense of what had happened. I brought some flowers and freshly baked pastries as a peace offering. I could at least remember outing my friends and propositioning them for a threesome. I suppose really I'd known that there was something going on for quite some time and I was happy for them, truly. I'd never meant to upset anyone. Ronan wasn't one to hold a grudge and forgave me instantly, gleefully tucking into the croissants as we sat at their kitchen table. Marc on the other hand, took a little more convincing.

'I just don't know why it had to be such a big secret' I said. 'You guys know we'd all be really happy for you.'

Marc glared at me while Ronan responded.

'The thing is Kerry, everyone else already knew. We just didn't want to make a big thing out of it because neither of us have had a boyfriend before and it was a bit unexpected. I knew you used to have a thing for Marc. I wasn't sure if you'd be upset. We just didn't want it to be a big deal...' He trailed off as Marc dutifully began making some coffee on the stove.

'I'm sorry, really I am' I said earnestly whilst also stinging with hurt from the realisation that someone who I now considered to be one of my closest friends thought I would be too jealous to rejoice in his happiness. *Was I really that untrustworthy?*

As we chatted a bit more, Marc softened towards me, even managing to crack a smile and I was able to piece together some more of what had happened.

'How did Anita know I'd slept with Erik?' I asked, not quite sure if I wanted to know the answer.

'Ah well, she didn't know that much, but she did see you kissing him in the Lord Lister' said Marc, a tone of pity entering his voice.

'Yeah, that's right' said Ronan, continuing the story. 'You saw him across the dancefloor and said you wanted to give him a piece of your mind, for Anita's sake. She tried to hold you back, but you couldn't be stopped...'

'And then' continued Marc, 'Somehow instead of punching him, you ended up kissing him in front of Anita.'

I buried my face in my hands. Hearing all of this was like peeling off a sticky plaster incredibly slowly, times a hundred.

'We weren't really sure what was going on with you guys, we were standing on the other side of the club when it happened but Anita ran out into the smoking area a little while later crying and so we took her home with us and she told us everything' Marc added.

Ronan nodded in solemn agreement.

'Yeah she was so upset' he said, before taking a sip of the espresso Marc had lovingly prepared for him.

My heart sank. Anita was so dear to me and had been nothing but a loving and loyal friend and it seemed I'd messed everything up.

'Right, I need to fix this' I said, suddenly rising to my feet.

'Hey steady on K-dog' said Ronan. 'Maybe just give her a few days to cool off.'

I could see the wisdom in his words, but my guilt and shame spoke louder.

As I left I turned once more to see Marc giving Ronan a peck on the cheek as he opened up the daily copy of Le Monde to peruse the politics pages.

'Hey guys, I really am happy for you, and I love you both, I mean it' I shouted across from the hall.

'We know' said Marc grinning. 'We love you too Kerry.'

'Even if you are a feckin' pain in the arse sometimes' jeered Ronan playfully.

I laughed as I closed the door behind me, satisfied that at least I'd managed to put out one small fire that I'd started.

So, you've dealt with the out-of-control chip pan. Now to deal with the raging inferno that is the rest of your live Kerry, no big deal. Let's do this.

***

Days passed and Anita wasn't answering the numerous texts and calls I'd made, the voicemails I'd left with fervent apologies and pleas of forgiveness. At this point I would have preferred anything. Even a one word reply or angry backlash would have been better than complete radio silence. I felt horrible.

I went into my final exam on Italian poetry barely able to concentrate.

As I wrote an adequate essay on Petrarch my thoughts periodically drifted to Anita, what she was doing, where she was. In the quiet of the exam hall the only sounds were pens eagerly scratching at paper, the occasional 'shush' or perplexed sigh. A bell rang to signal the end of the exam. My studies in Bologna were over.

I decided to mark the occasion by taking a trip to my favourite gelato spot, the one where the middle-aged balding proprietor always gave me extra strawberry sauce with a wink and no extra charge. I sat inside and looked out over the view of Piazza Santo Stefano with its historic ochre basilica. Pigeons cooed and ruffled their feathers in its high arches while down below other students sat on benches, notebooks open as they tested one another.

I hid behind a menu as I saw James walk past. He was holding hands with a pretty Italian woman with glossy chestnut hair. She wore a polka dot dress and smart blazer, so I presumed she was also a teacher and looked to be around his age. It felt like a dagger was piercing my heart. *So, this was really why he broke up with me*?

All this time I'd thought James was the model man, the perfect gentleman but it turned out he was just like the rest of them; spineless and cowardly. At least Edward didn't try to hide his true nature by pretending to be something he wasn't. Still, I couldn't deny that James was smiling and did seem genuinely happy. *Maybe everyone was just better off with me out of the picture?*

James and I hadn't discussed the future. I suppose our relationship was over before it had even begun. But I would have been willing to try long distance. I gathered that he wanted to stay in Bologna for the foreseeable future. Cheap flights back and forth to Italy from Manchester were easy to come by. We could have made it work. But it seemed he didn't think we had something that was worth fighting for. He didn't think *I* was worth the effort. This was a painful truth to swallow.

I ordered more ice cream and stayed there for quite a while, wallowing in my misfortune as I doodled images of flowers, cats and love hearts on the napkins. Then the sky grew dark, and a shower erupted, causing the people in the square to scatter, seeking shelter in the nearby arches and porticoes as they held books above their heads to keep dry. I knew it wouldn't last. It was late June so the weather had started to become quite hot. But sometimes the increased humidity could give way to thunderstorms.

I hung around as long as I could in the hopes that it would ease off but it only seemed to get heavier and I felt I would be sick if I ate any more strawberry gelato. I decided to make a dash for it, taking refuge in the doorway of the Basilica.

One of the best things about Bologna was that when it did rain, the network of arcades meant it was easy to stay relatively dry so I plotted my way home under them, taking a slightly longer route as roars of thunder echoed off the buildings and flashes of lightning illuminated the grey sky.

I came across a quaint independent bookshop with rows of neatly arranged volumes of all kinds of books in the window and decided to have a look inside. I wasn't in any rush to get home. I knew Barbara would be there since she'd taken a few days off work and as much as I wanted to comfort her I just didn't know what to say.

My only experience of grief so far had been losing my granny when I was at school, but she'd been 85 years old, struggling with Dementia and it was easier to accept because she'd lived a long life. It was her time. I couldn't imagine what it must be like to lose a friend for good, feeling as though you've been cheated out of so many more memories together.

I perused the different sections, flicking through some non-fiction on post-feminism, reading the synopsises on the back of a few romance novels. The beady eyed woman at the counter eyed me suspiciously over her heavy rimmed glasses from behind the counter, probably wondering if I intended to buy anything. As much as I'd tried in the past to enjoy more 'serious' books, I almost always inevitably ending up checking out some chick-lit, when I went to the library. If I couldn't have a happy ending of my own, I could at least read about one.

As I rounded the corner of one of the shelves I saw Anita, flicking through an art book on the Italian renaissance. She was so engrossed in it that she didn't notice me until I was right beside her.

'Hi' I said sheepishly.

She turned and looked right through me as though I didn't exist before putting the book back and swiftly making her way to the door. I shuffled after her, following her out into the storm.

'Listen it didn't mean anything, I was drunk' I said, grabbing her shoulder.

'That's not an excuse' she seethed, a look of pure hatred in her eyes.

'I know. But you broke up ages ago. I didn't think you still had feelings for him.'

'That's not the point.'

'I know' I said, lowering my eyes in shame.

'Don't touch me' she said, shaking off my hand.

'I suppose you slept with him as well did you?' she said accusatorily.

I looked away not wanting to admit it. For a moment, silence hung between us like a lead weight as the rain got heavier. My clothes stuck to my skin.

'You're a slut' she hissed.

Her words stung like acid.

'You don't mean that' I said, in a strained whimper.

But what if she did? What if she was right?

She turned and walked away in a red-faced fury. It was only as I put my hand to my face that I realised I was crying, my tears blending with the rain.

***

A few weeks passed and there was still no sight or sound of Anita. I knew she was meeting up with Marc and Ronan separately, but they were both unwilling to tell me much about her when I saw them, not wanting to get involved.

'Look Kerry, this is between you and her, said Ronan diplomatically. 'Just give it time, I'm sure she'll come round.'

Unfortunately, patience wasn't one of my strong suits. I'd been so distracted by the fall-out with Anita that it was a while before I realised my period was significantly late that month. I panicked. I hadn't wanted the gory details from my night with Edward, but I presumed that in our inebriated state it was likely we didn't take the necessary precautions.

I really wished I could go back in time and just change everything, but I couldn't. I knew that if I'd been sober, I never would have touched Edward with a barge pole. But I wasn't. I was lonely, sad, drunk and on the rebound. I didn't want to make excuses for myself, but I hadn't been in any state to give consent and if Edward was a half decent guy he would have known that. He even had the audacity to text me one night around midnight for a booty call. I told him to go fuck himself. That was one mistake I didn't intent to repeat.

I confided in Ronan about my predicament while we were eating pizza in Piazza Verdi one night. It was just the two of us since Marc was away in Rome for a few nights attending some special philosophy convention. I loved hanging out with them as a couple, but I was also glad to have some quality time one on one with Ronan.

'Oh, shit Kerry, I suppose you'd better take a test' he said, whilst messily folding a slice of pizza marinara into his mouth.

'I know' I said, 'But I'm scared.'

'I get it' said Ronan. If anyone was going to understand the potential moral quandry I'd be facing it would be Ronan.

'But you'll have to find out sooner or later.'

I knew he was right.

As I cycled home via Via dell'independenza I spotted a woman sitting at a fold-out table covered in a silk cloth. She was shuffling a card deck with an array of colourful scenes on them. I peered curiously at her, and she caught my eye, beckoning me over with her bejewelled hand. As I drew closer she adjusted the Indigo scarf around her shoulders and motioned for me to sit down. She was quite old, with grey whiskers growing out of her wrinkled chin but her eyes sparkled with a youthful vitality. An array of crystals were arranged on the table next to her cards. They glinted in the glow of an antique copper lantern she was using, the flame gently flickering behind a glass encasing that was hand painted with a moon and stars. I tentatively took a seat on the wooden stool not quite knowing what was going to happen.

'So, Kerry' she said. 'Would you like a reading?'

'Uh, yes. Wait, how do you know my name?'

'I have my ways' she said knowingly, tapping her nose with her finger. She wore many shiny gold bangles with jangled when she moved her hands. It was quite a pleasing sound.

'I don't know how this works' I confessed, squirming a little on my seat.

'That's fine, let's begin' she said as she shuffled the cards and cut the deck in half.

She asked me to pick a pile and then shuffled that once more before drawing three cards and laying them in front of her.

'Hmm, interesting' she said. 'You're in the midst of a conflict with someone very dear to you' she mused, pointing to an image on one of the cards which depicted a man on a boat rowing with a huddled figure and six swords. 'But this will soon be coming to an end.'

My eyes lit up. I wasn't sure if I believed in all this 'woo woo' stuff but I really wanted that to be true.

'You have some good friends, they are your closest allies and advisors' she said, pointing to a card showing three figures standing below a stone arch carved with a design of three pentacles. 'But you mustn't take them for granted or you will lose them' she said in a serious tone.

I nodded. The final card depicted a knight on a white horse holding a golden cup.

'You will soon have an offer of love being made. But this will not be the only choice you have to make. Think wisely before you accept it, there are many paths available to you at this time.'

I frowned, wishing she could be more specific.

'Is there anything else you wish to know my child?' she asked finally, regarding me with a sage expression.

I thought for a moment before answering. There were a lot of questions I could ask but I wasn't sure if I wanted to know the answers.

'No that is fine thank you' I said as I lay a 10 euro note on the table for payment.

Before I left she grabbed my hand unexpectedly and I flinched.

'Just remember Kerry' she said. 'White knights can come in all shapes and sizes.'

I nodded as she released her grip even though I wasn't quite sure what she meant.

Chapter 20

I finally got up the courage to take a pregnancy test. Buying one from the chemist had been mortifying.

'Buona Suerte' said the kind old cashier with a knowing wink as he popped it in a paper bag for me. Why were the Italians obsessed with me having a child? I wasn't ready on any level - emotionally, physically or spiritually. I could just about look after myself and that was hard enough. How on earth did the Virgin Mary cope? She did everything right and still managed to get up the duff!

I rushed straight to the bathroom when I got home, not even pausing to greet Barbara who was busying herself in the kitchen as usual. Everyone had their own way of dealing with grief and hers took the form of cooking. Non-stop cooking. If I wasn't pregnant I'd soon look it from all the tagliatelle, bolognese, ricotta filled tortellini, pancetta, panna cotta, tiramisu... I felt it was my duty as a friend to eat for two (pregnant or otherwise) as sign of my support at this difficult time. Even if I felt sick afterwards, it was worth it to see the smile on Barbara's face when I said *'Brava, Buonissimo!'* and she'd beam at the sight of my empty plate.

Once on the toilet, I spared no time in unwrapping my fated package and unceremoniously peeing on the stick. It seemed bizarre that my entire future could be decided by the outcome of a wee. *Please be negative, please, please, please, pretty please God...*

I wasn't the best Catholic, but I was good enough to know that abortion wasn't an option. I knew I'd either be leaving that bathroom with all my hopes and dreams for the future intact or I'd be planning how to co-parent with Edward. Eugh! *Maybe he wouldn't want anything to do with it? Yes that would be a lot better.*

Aside from the fact that he had an utterly repulsive personality I didn't really know a lot about him or his family. What if he had some sort of rare genetic disorder and our child came out with tusks or a tail? They'd be bullied relentlessly at school and I'd have to drop out of uni for at least a year and everyone would laugh at me and even if they didn't seem to be mocking me, I know they'd be talking about me behind my back and commenting on how stupid I was, 'Imagine getting pregnant unexpectedly in this day and age' they'd say. 'What a trollop!'

And of course, my mum would disown me, so I'd be forced to move to some distant land, set up home in a cave or something, just me and my strangely deformed child. Of course, I'd love him or her in my own way but a part of me would always resent them and they'd sense this and grow up with cripplingly low self-esteem and eventually turn to heroin or a life of crime…

It was the moment of truth. I held my breath as I looked at the test.

One thin red line.

I immediately cried tears of relief. *Thank you God, thank you thank you thank you. I owe you one!*

Barbara overheard and rushed to my aid.

'Kerry, what's wrong? *C'è un problema?*' she asked concernedly through the bathroom door.

'No, no I'm fine. Uh, just cut myself shaving' I replied. She had enough on her plate (in every sense) to worry about me and my philandering.

***

To celebrate the end of exams we'd decided to have a big night out. I was determined to enjoy myself to the max now that I knew I didn't have to worry about premature motherhood. I'd given myself a stern pep-talk. *Just make sure you don't sleep with anyone tonight Kerry, for the love of all that's holy.*

In an effort to not drink too much and achieve a charming level of tipsy without crossing over into shamefully paralytic or blackout I decided to leave my bank card at home and only take out a ten euro note. *What's the worst that could happen from only drinking ten euros worth of booze?*

We met as usual in Piazza Verdi and from there headed down to Via del Pratello where we did a crawl of our favourite haunts. It was the first time I'd seen Anita in a couple of weeks and as much as the others denied it, I think she was still purposefully avoiding me. Once I'd even gone round to her place in an attempt to make peace, but Tatiana had greeted me at the door in a black satin dressing gown, blocking my view of the hallway, and mumbling some excuse that Anita was studying late at the library and wouldn't be back till later. She was a terrible liar.

I thought forgiveness might come from having a bit of distance, but she still seemed quite icy towards me, only addressing me so I could pass a beer to Ronan or to request a light. I didn't smoke but I'd taken to always carrying a lighter in my handbag in case anyone needed it.

Some Italian students were graduating so we saw a lot of them out and about in the bars, adorned with traditional laurel wreathes on their heads and black capes. It seemed the most acceptable way to celebrate three years of academic achievement at a renowned institution was to get blind drunk, dance till your feet hurt and puke on the pavement, before eventually staggering home.

As the night went on Anita seemed to soften in her attitude towards me although the copious amount of rosé she was drinking probably helped. Despite my plan not to drink too much, everyone was in a celebratory mood, so I ended up receiving quite a lot of free drinks and shots both from fellow students and the people working behind the bars. One good looking guy in a crisp suit winked at me from across the dancefloor and we danced for a bit before he offered to buy me a whiskey. I accepted the drink but then promptly ditched him, not wanting to get into any more compromising situations.

At one club I stepped outside to get a breath of fresh air and saw a muscly looking guy having an altercation with Anita. His hands were clasped around her slender throat, and she was struggling to breathe. In a flash of anger, I dashed towards them and ordered him to stop, wasting no time in kicking him in the balls. He promptly let go of Anita as he winced in pain and doubled over on the kerb. It seemed I hadn't been the only one to take a hit at him that night since he already had a black eye and an ugly scar on his puffy lip. I quickly led Anita away into the empty square nearby and we sat on a bench whilst she regained her composure.

'Thanks Kerry' she said finally once she'd got her breath back. 'That son of a bitch just wouldn't take 'No' for an answer.'

Apart from some faint red marks around her neck she seemed to be otherwise physically unharmed.

'You're welcome' I said softly as I ventured to hold her hand. I didn't want to say too much for fear of ruining this potential chance for reconciliation.

After a period of silence broken only by the distant hum of music and the screeching of some cats fighting I said, 'Anita, I'm so sorry, I mean it. I never meant to hurt you.'

She looked at me, her perfect face illuminated by the amber glow of a streetlamp.

'I know' she said, shuffling a bit closer to me. 'I wasn't upset because I still had feelings for Edward. I was mad because you'd put yourself in a dangerous scenario and I care about you Kerry' she said tenderly as she touched my cheek. 'I just wished you would take better care of yourself.'

I started to cry tears of relief as I was humbled by her kindness. The truth was I didn't think I was worthy of it. I didn't think I deserved to have a friend like her.

I helped Anita to get a taxi home soon after since she no longer was in the mood to party and I couldn't blame her. I rejoined the others and despite my best efforts managed to get more and more inebriated as the night went on. In the end I was dancing on the bar and being a general nuisance by falling down, knocking over other people's drinks and being offensive without meaning to. The last thing I remembered was getting separated from the others and smashing a wine glass before being thrown out of the club by the burly black-clad bouncer.

***

I woke up to the sound of nearby traffic and pigeons cooing and rustling about my head. The smell of drain water mixed with the aroma of freshly baked bread wafted in my direction. I wasn't in my own bed. *Shit!* Or any bed for that matter.

It seemed I was on the cold hard cobbles of an alleyway behind a bakery. I'd spend the night on the street. *Double shit!* What's more, when I looked in my bag the zip was broken and my phone and purse were gone, leaving only a few receipts for various bars, my lipstick and a half-finished packet of chewing gum.

My lighter was also missing but it seemed I'd accidentally set my hair alight at some point since the ends were lightly singed. *Triple shit!* My mind immediately sprang into action like a court jester, conjuring up ideas and jokes so I could brush this off as another 'Kerry just being an eegit' moment and spin it as a humorous tale to tell my friends.

But my heart sank as I knelt down next to a pile of rubbish and tried to resist the urge to vomit. I knew I couldn't do that this time. There was nothing glamorous or funny about this scenario. I couldn't keep pretending that everything was fine when it clearly wasn't. This was more than just a phase or a symptom of youth. It was time to face the truth. I had a problem.

After stumbling home, drinking copious amounts of water, showering, cancelling my bank cards and sleeping for a few hours in my own bed, I awoke with a clear resolve to get some help. If I carried on at this rate I was going to be dead before the age of 25. And as challenging as life could be at times, I certainly didn't want that. There was of course the one positive to dying young in that maybe I'd have the opportunity to come back as a ghost and haunt Edward by writing messages in the steamed-up mirror like 'You're a nob.' But that was only a slight possibility.

If I died I wanted to go peacefully and painlessly in my sleep at a grand old age with my loved ones keeping vigil at my bedside or conversely doing something cool like swimming with sharks or climbing Mount Everest. I certainly didn't want my epitaph to read, 'She died doing what she loved; drinking copious amounts of whiskey and cheap red wine whilst falling off a bar stool in an effort to get up and dance the Macarena.' No, I wanted my legacy to be pithier and much less tragic.

So, this is how I found myself in a basement under a bookshop on a hot summer's evening in Bologna. The lights were painfully bright so there was nowhere to hide, and I shifted uncomfortably in my plastic fold-out chair as people of all ages, shapes and sizes tried their best to offer me reassuring smiles and welcome me by placing a reassuring hand on my back or insisting I have first pick of the biscotti. I averted their eyes as I nursed my fennel tisane in its white plastic cup, determined not to cry but failing miserably as tears stubbornly trickled down my cheeks.

I could have asked someone to come with me for moral support. But for some reason that seemed harder, as though having a witness to my lowest ebb would somehow make it more real. Plus, I felt I'd already caused enough upset and inconvenience. I didn't want to burden anyone or push the limits of my friends' kindness. I sat in a circle as I listened to stories of hardship and pain, of what alcohol had cost these people or taken away from them; friends, family, homes, jobs. But these were also tales of bravery, redemption and hope.

They were mostly locals who spoke in Italian, but a few expats shared in English whilst another member of the group translated for them. I was surprised that it wasn't just all wrinkly old men with bad breath. One woman who'd moved to Italy from the US several years prior shared how she'd built a life and business in Bologna, working as an artist. She'd got married and raised two children, but she lost it all due to her drinking, eventually ending up homeless, penniless and divorced with no access to her daughters. I could scarcely reconcile the person she described with the person who sat before me now with slick blond hair, shiny pink lacquered nails and a glowing smile. She was the picture of health and sanity. Whilst I was crippled with regret, shame and despair, I could see that she had been liberated from these evils.

One man, dressed impeccably in an Armani suit, offered me a silk handkerchief from his pocket to blow my nose on. When I tried to return it, he smiled warmly and insisted I keep it. To this day it stays in a box with my most treasured keepsakes.

I thought I'd be the youngest person there but at the end a couple of students around my age invited me to a special young person's meeting the following evening and we exchanged phone numbers. 'It gets better' they said. 'Just take it one day at a time.'

It felt like a monumental task to vow to never drink again. How would I get through Christmases, birthdays, St Patrick's day? But resolving not to drink just for that day seemed manageable.

I cycled home and as I passed the cathedral in the main square flocks of swallows flitted in and out of the eaves, creating a pleasing cacophony. I breathed in the sweet warm air, feeling a newfound lightness in my being. I knew that no matter how hard it would be, no matter what anxieties and fears my mind conjured up, everything really was going to be okay in the end.

Chapter 21

'Hey, wait for me, I yelled' as Ronan bounded ahead of me, taking the steps two at a time.

'Get a move on, it's not that far' he shouted back.

We were climbing up under a roofed arcade through six hundred and sixty-six arches to San Luca; a church perched on top of a hill that promised a spectacular view of Bologna. We'd been meaning to take the pilgrimage for ages but just hadn't got round to it. I thought back to that day when we'd gone up Torre Asinelli. So much had happened since then, so much had changed that it felt like a lifetime ago. Time is funny like that.

As I panted in the mid-July heat I thought about all the things and people I was going to miss. Friends, sunshine, the pizza, the laughter, aperitivo, espresso, even Barbara and her mad ways. She'd gone away to visit family in Sicily and wouldn't be back before I left so we'd already said our teary goodbyes. Her parting gift to me was a diary with a picture of Mussolini on the front.

I made sure to finish my mural and bid farewell to all the people at the Communist squatters' building. They praised my art and wished me well for the future as we shared one last joint and talked nonsense about love, life, aliens and government conspiracy. I hoped that one day I'd return to that place and be able to show the mural to my children as proof that I'd been cool once. I did in fact go back but unsurprisingly the only evidence of my rebellious youth had been long since erased by several layers of paint.

When we finally reached the summit, the others were already there waiting for us, languidly sprawled out on the lawn in front of the modest terracotta basilica.

'Ah finally!' said Anita with mock annoyance as she jumped up to greet us. I kissed her in the Italian way, overflowing with gratitude that things were back to normal between us. She was radiant in a pinstriped sundress, a garland of daisies on her head. And while I was a sweaty, stinky mess she smelt like vanilla and fresh-cut rosemary.

'What took you so long?' asked Tatiana. She twisted her ring nonchalantly which glittered in the sun as she lay with knees bent, her head in Erik's lap.

'This one' replied Ronan, poking me playfully in the ribs, 'Utter slow coach.'

I feigned offence and laughed as we sat down next to the others.

'So, what now?' asked Marc, lifting his sunglasses. He was impeccably dressed as always in a short-sleeved navy shirt and beige cotton shorts. I wondered how on earth he had managed to climb all the way up there seemingly without breaking a sweat.

'I brought some drinks' said Ronan as I caught my breath. It would have seemed disrespectful to drink alcohol in front of the church so he'd filled some coca-cola bottles with one part vodka.

'What a legend!' said Erik as Ronan passed him one from the cool bag.

I twitched and wrung my hands together as the craving struck me like a hot iron, a whip of both pleasure and pain, but I rode the wave and it passed. I would stick to my lemonade. I would not give in. When I'd told the others of my decision to stop drinking I thought they'd be surprised but the overwhelming sentiment was relief and support.

Even though they also drank heavily it seemed I was the one who always just took it a bit too far and it hadn't gone unnoticed. Anita in particular said she was proud of me and that meant a lot. She even came with me to some of my group recovery meetings for moral support.

'No, I meant what are your plans for the future? What happens when you all leave Bologna?' said Marc.

We all fell silent for a moment. A waning moon was visible in the clear blue sky like a smudge of chalk, unnaturally revealing itself in the daylight.

'Well, straight back to Russia for me' said Anita wistfully with a loving sideways glance at the happy couple. Tatiana was going travelling with Erik around Europe so the girls would be going their separate ways until the end of the summer. I knew we'd all be invited to the wedding, but I'd been doing Anita's head in, pestering her to ask Tatiana if they'd set a date or location yet. I loved an excuse to get dressed up all fancy.

'Yes, we're going interrailing, we just want to explore and have as much fun as we can before we need to get back to studying hard' chirped Erik. 'If we're going to spend the rest of our lives together the adventure may as well begin now' he added as he tenderly cupped his fiancée's face in his hands.

Anita winked at me, and I choked back a laugh as I sipped my lemonade. The sugary tanginess of it gave me a head rush.

'I'm going to head straight back to Dublin, spend some time with the family, maybe go fishing with me Da' said Ronan.

He swigged his drink while picking absent-mindedly at the lush grass.

I didn't really know what to say. I'd purposefully tried to avoid thinking about tomorrow when I'd be heading on a flight back to Northern Ireland. I'd have a month with my mother, half of which would be spent arguing about my future and the rest drinking tea and watching reality TV. She did my head in sometimes, but I missed her and the cats. I didn't really want to return to my normal everyday life though, especially not my final year at uni. I'd need to study hard and pick a career path. God knows I wasn't ready for it. I wanted more time. I wanted to stay in this unreal bubble of paradise for just a little bit longer. But I knew I couldn't.

In the end I expertly dodged the question by pointing out how beautiful the sky looked and all the landmarks that could be seen down below. Marc smirked, clearly noticing my avoidance but he didn't push me further.

'What about you Marc? What's next for you *mon cheri*?' said Anita, impishly tilting her head to the side.

'Well, I don't know, we'll see' he replied. His eyes briefly lingered on Ronan who returned his gaze with a wry smile. I was happy if they were happy but like some 18th century Lord of the manor who fretted over his daughters' wellbeing, I hoped Marc's intentions were truly honourable. I didn't want to see a good friend get hurt.

We all stayed there talking and enjoying the glorious view as we watched the sun dip below the horizon, bathing us in golden light. Anita held my hand as we skipped back down the steps whilst she attempted to teach me a Russian folk song.

I blushed as I fumbled over the words. My brain was a little bit fuzzier than normal even though I was completely sober. The heat and the bittersweet knowledge that all good things must come to an end swam around my mind, competing for attention.

'It's called *Kalinka* and it's about a 'little berry' which is a metaphor for a beautiful woman…just like you' she said, pinching me playfully in the soft skin of my inner arm. I was going to miss her terribly.

'Hey, maybe you could come and visit me in Ireland sometime, I mean, if you'd like that too?'

Her eyes sparkled as she smiled.

'I thought you'd never ask.'

***

The night before I was due to leave Bologna I packed my bags, carefully stowing away the keepsakes I'd accumulated – a beer mat from The Emerald, my Christmas gifts, the programme from the Opera, an Erasmus club night wristband, train tickets to Ravenna and Verona. I paused for a moment when I came to my beautiful garnet pendant. I'd debated whether or not to keep it. It seemed tainted now, like James had only given it to me in order to assuage his guilt, but at the same time I really did love it. I'd been so angry at the time but now I realised that James and I just weren't meant to be in the long term, and I'd come to accept that. In the end I chose not to part with it, carefully stowing it in the inner pocket of my handbag which I'd be taking on the plane.

Alone in my blue room, I fired up my laptop to check my emails, just in case there were any important notices from uni I'd forgotten about.

I had one message in my inbox:

From: Juliet's Secretaries

Subject: Reply to 'Advice Please'

Buon Giorno Kerry,

Apologies for the delay in replying to your message, as you can imagine we receive a lot of enquiries.

You asked if I believe that two people can be 'fated' to be together (like Julliet and Romeo) and if so, how can one ascertain if someone is 'the one.' You also wonder if true love is apparent straight away or if it can be more gradual and grow over time.

In response I can say that yes, I do believe in 'star-crossed lovers' but that we also have the power and free will to choose who we love. I do believe that we all have a special someone who is out there waiting to be found. But I also know that in a lot of cases that special someone may be right in front of us but we're oblivious to them because we've fallen in love gradually over time without even noticing.

This may be the case for you. True love is someone who is always there for you, someone who will fight your corner no matter what, someone you can laugh with and cry with, share the highs and lows of life with. True love isn't just someone who's willing to agree and go along with everything you say, but someone who's willing to challenge you also, and support you to be the best possible version of yourself. True love doesn't always come with grand romantic gestures and fireworks. Sometimes it can simply be a listening ear or a shoulder to cry on. Does any of this sound familiar? In my experience rarely have I seen a person who is truly in love who has cause to doubt their connection, even when they experience great challenges or hardships, and the odds seem stacked against them.

If you have doubts about this 'James' already I would suggest that he isn't 'the one' for you. True love isn't something you can rationalise intellectually in your mind even if someone seems 'perfect' on paper or appears to tick all the boxes To find true love, one must always follow their heart.

I hope this helps.

Love always,

Secretaries of Juliet Xx

Early August, 2016 – Giant's Causeway, N.Ireland

Chapter 22

She touched my arm lightly as we paused at the cliff edge, stopping to gaze out at the Atlantic. For Ireland, it was a pleasant enough summer's day but a cool wind nipped my cheeks and tousled my hair. Below us the waves whipped against hexagonal rock formations, uniquely forged from volcanic lava as tourists of all nationalities scrambled around them like ants.

As I stared out at the vast expanse of stormy ocean, I thought back to my midnight swim at Ravenna, how warm and inviting the water had been. It was hard to believe that was almost two years ago.

'Money for your thoughts?' said Anita, smirking up at me with a curious look in her eyes.

'It's a penny' I corrected.

'Well, that's cheap, they can't be very interesting' she giggled.

'No, I mean the saying in English is 'A penny for your thoughts.'

'Oh.'

We both laughed and huddled closer together, crinkling the fabric of our waterproof coats.

I was glad Anita had come to visit. In just two weeks I was set to start a new job in London, working as a translator for the Italian Embassy. It didn't feel real. Adulthood beckoned me with the prospect of early nights and sensible shoes. I wasn't ready. University had come and gone in a whirlwind and all I had left to show for it was a stiff sheet of paper. It wasn't enough. I wanted something to quell the crippling doubts that sometimes bubbled below my can-do veneer, someone to hold my hand and tell me that everything was going to be ok.

In those moments of abject fear, all I wanted was to be back at Piazza Verdi, sipping cheap Peronis and not thinking about tomorrow. But I'd been sober for nearly two years, I was proud of the progress I'd made and when those stray thoughts of a drink crept in I had to remind myself where that 'one drink' would always lead me.

Now I woke up every day with a clear head in a dry bed. I could always remember every detail of the night before and I didn't lose precious sections of my life to the abyss of blackout. I no longer self-sabotaged my relationships and opportunities. Although not drinking meant that my fears, anxieties and inner critic were sometimes a bit louder, it also meant that every day, one day at a time I was turning up the dial on my inner peace, joy, serenity and courage. God, I sound like a motivational poster from the library!

She took my hand in hers and gently brushed a stray curl away from my face. The scene was almost serene if not for the roar of waves crashing against the cliff face and the shriek of gulls circling overhead. She leant forward and I felt her warm breath on my cheek.

'Close your eyes' she whispered.

'Why?' I asked, raising an eyebrow.

'Because I said so.'

I relented, shutting out the bright sun that was now beginning to dip below the horizon.

Then she kissed me, her soft lips gently pressing against mine with an ardent desire. At first, I flinched, but only briefly. I gripped her waist, pulling her closer to me in a warm embrace as the wind continued to whirl around us.

'Anita' I uttered softly, breaking away from our kiss.

'Yes?' she said, pressing a warm palm against my cheek.

'I love you'

'I love you too'

The words melted in the air like a wisp of sweet incense, filling my heart with the warm glow of ecstasy. As I stood upon land that legend has it was once inhabited by Giants, I felt ten feet tall.

And in that moment, it all made sense. All the heartbreak and despair, all the laughter and the tears. Every step in the dance of life had brought me closer to her and I knew that given half the chance I'd do it all again.